‾ P A

||| ||| |||| |||||||||| |||||||| ||||| ||| |||

WITHDRAWN ✔ **KT-426-343**

....

**PLEASE RETURN TO THE ABOVE LIBRARY OR ANY OTHER ABERDEEN
CITY LIBRARY, ON OR BEFORE THE DUE DATE. TO RENEW, PLEASE
QUOTE THE DUE DATE AND THE BARCODE NUMBER.**

 Aberdeen City Council
Library & Information Services   ♻

X000 000 040 2500

||||| |||||| || ||||| ||| ||||| ||||| |||||||| |||| |||

ABERDEEN CITY LIBRARIES

BLACK MOONLIGHT

A MARJORIE MCCLELLAND MYSTERY

BLACK MOONLIGHT

AMY PATRICIA MEADE

WHEELER
CHIVERS

This Large Print edition is published by Wheeler Publishing, Waterville, Maine, USA and by AudioGO Ltd, Bath, England.
Wheeler Publishing, a part of Gale, Cengage Learning.

LIBRARY OF CONGRESS CATALOGING-IN-PUBLICATION DATA

Meade, Amy Patricia, 1972–
    Black moonlight : a Marjorie McClelland mystery / by Amy Patrick Meade.
        p. cm. — (Wheeler Publishing large print cozy mystery)
    ISBN-13: 978-1-4104-3130-1 (pbk.)
    ISBN-10: 1-4104-3130-4 (pbk.)
    1. McClelland, Marjorie (Fictitious character)—Fiction. 2. Women novelists—Fiction. 3. Upper class families—England—Fiction. 4. English—Bermuda Islands—Fiction. 5. Bermuda Islands—Fiction. 6. Murder—Investigation—Fiction. 7. Large type books. I. Title.
    PS3613.E128B53 2010b
    813'.6—dc22   2010031480

BRITISH LIBRARY CATALOGUING-IN-PUBLICATION DATA AVAILABLE

Published in 2010 in the U.S. by arrangement with Midnight Ink, an imprint of Llewellyn Publications, Woodbury, MN 55125-2989 USA.
Published in 2011 in the U.K. by arrangement with Llewellyn Worldwide, Ltd.

U.K. Hardcover: 978 1 408 49341 0 (Chivers Large Print)
U.K. Softcover: 978 1 408 49342 7 (Camden Large Print)

Printed in the United States of America
1 2 3 4 5 6 7 14 13 12 11 10

BLACK MOONLIGHT

ONE

"That's extortion!" 75-year-old Emily Patterson cried from the back room of Schutt's Book Nook.

"No, that's restitution," corrected Walter Schutt, the store's wizened proprietor. "We were going to throw them the wedding to end all weddings. The least they could do is pay us back for all our hard work."

"And the supplies we purchased," added Walter's wife, Louise. "I bought enough ingredients to make Perfection Salad for the entire town!"

Mrs. Patterson drew a deep breath. The Schutts could always be depended upon to use the First Presbyterian Church board meetings as their platform for condemning the wrongdoings of their Ridgebury, Connecticut, brethren, but never were they so outspoken as when they were "sponsoring" the gatherings. ("Sponsoring" being the operative word, since the provision of an unheated storage room, a card table, a few folding chairs, a pitcher of water, and a plate of dry, heavy pound cake could not be defined as "hosting" or "hospitality" any more than Louise Schutt's Perfection Salad could be described as "delicious.")

"I'm certain they would have appreciated your efforts, Mrs. Schutt," reasoned the fourth, and final, participant of the afternoon's meeting, the always-affable gray-haired cleric, Reverend Price. "But you know how young people in love can be. Impetuous."

"Impetuous?" Mrs. Schutt folded a set of beefy arms across her ample chest. "Impolite is more like it!"

"Inconsiderate, even," Mr. Schutt chimed in.

Never were the Schutts so infuriating as when they believed they were the subjects of some personal affront — in this case, the elopement of the town's most celebrated couple: mystery writer and part-time detective, Marjorie McClelland, and British millionaire, Creighton Ashcroft.

"I hardly think a case of lemon gelatin is going to spoil, Louise," Mrs. Patterson retorted. "As for your canned pickles and pimentos, I daresay they would have survived the Battle of Verdun."

"And what about the cabbage?" Mrs. Schutt challenged. "My Perfection Salad calls for one half a head of cabbage, shredded. I bought three heads. What am I supposed to do with those?"

"It's August," the older woman shrugged. "Make coleslaw."

"Why, Emily Patterson, I'm surprised by your attitude! I know you think of Marjorie as the daughter you never had, but to defend her behavior . . . well!"

"This is 1935, Louise. Young women are no longer bound by our Victorian ideas of marriage and etiquette; they're writing mystery novels and piloting themselves across the Atlantic." Mrs. Patterson sighed. "Am I disappointed that I didn't get to give Marjorie a wedding? Of course I am. But when Marjorie called from the ship, she sounded completely over the moon. My joy at her happiness far exceeds any disappointment I may feel."

Reverend Price cleared his throat. "I don't profess to know much about wedding receptions and the social niceties surrounding them   I leave those things to you and the other ladies in our congregation. However, why couldn't we throw Marjorie and Creighton a reception upon their return? That way Mrs. Patterson can rejoice with

9

the two people she cares about and, Mrs. Schutt, um, well, your cabbage won't go to waste."

Mrs. Schutt drew a hand to her chest in an exaggerated gesture of shock and horror. "A wedding? They're already married!"

"No, not a 'wedding', per se," the Reverend explained, "but a secular celebration of their new life together."

"I think it's a lovely idea," Mrs. Patterson spoke up. "We could stick with the same menu we had planned for the reception, but change the decorations to something more 'welcome home' in nature. They would be delighted!"

Mrs. Schutt, however, would not be swayed. "I think it's an appalling idea. They ran off and eloped with nary a second thought as to our plans, and now you're going to reward them with a surprise party?" She clicked her tongue loudly. "Well, you can leave Walter and me out of it. Can't they, Walter?"

At this question, a daydreaming Mr. Schutt snapped to life. "Hmm? Oh, yes. Why, certainly. It's an absurd idea."

"Then I suppose you'll have to stuff it," Mrs. Patterson concluded.

The color rose in Mrs. Schutt's plump cheeks. "What!" she nearly shrieked.

10

"Your cabbage," Emily Patterson calmly explained. "If you're not bringing your Perfection Salad to the party, you'll have to find something to do with the three heads you bought. I had a friend in Norwalk who used to make stuffed cabbage; she's passed on now, but as I recall, it's a very tasty dish."

"Oh!" Mrs. Schutt exclaimed as she extracted a lace-trimmed hankie from her bosom and proceeded to fan herself with it. "I cannot believe we're having this discussion. They knew how much thought we had put into this wedding, but they went ahead and eloped just the same. And let's not forget what Mr. Ashcroft did to our dear, sweet, wonderful Sharon!" She shook her head, "No, I cannot participate in this party. I've been left to deal with three heads of cabbage, a case of lemon gelatin, and a spinster daughter, while they're off in the Atlantic having a gay old time. Why, they're probably 'whooping it up' as we speak!"

TWO

Marjorie lay down upon the bed and looked beseechingly at Creighton. "Will I ever be able to eat solid food again?" she asked with a soft burp.

Creighton poured a glass of water from the bedside pitcher and handed it to his new bride. "You'll be fine once we dock in Hamilton. In the meantime, the ship's doctor gave me these for you to take." He placed two white pills on her open palm.

"Will these get rid of my sea sickness?" she asked eagerly.

"From my experience, they'll either stop the symptoms completely or make you so sleepy that you can't tell whether you're queasy or not."

Marjorie swallowed the pills and chased it with a mouthful of water. "You mean I'm going to be knocked out," she paraphrased.

"More or less," Creighton shrugged.

Marjorie sat up on her elbows. "But it's

12

our honeymoon. I don't want to be drugged. I've never been abroad before."

"Don't worry, darling," Creighton assured. "You'll only be knocked out for the day, and we have plenty of honeymoon left. Actually, when we get to Hamilton, I have something special in store for you."

She eased back and let her head flop onto the pillow. "Creighton, darling, you used that line last night, and although it was cute the first time —"

"Not that type of surprise," he interrupted. "My family owns an island, off the coast of Bermuda, just a few miles from Hamilton. How about we leave this bucket of bolts behind and spend a week by the sea — just the two of us?"

"Are you kidding? I'd give my right arm to be off this ship. But won't the rest of your family be there? I mean, your father —"

Creighton shook his head. "No. Mother left the place to him, but he never enjoyed it the way she did. Growing up, we'd spend the month of March or April there."

"Why? Does the airplane manufacturing business shut down in March or April?"

"Funny. No, we went to escape the cold and wet of England and New York. Mother's been gone nearly twenty-five years now and the old man still goes there the same time

13

every year." He shook his head and frowned. "On the bright side, my father's annoying need for uniformity ensures that he will not be anywhere near the place. Ah, think of it, darling! Pink sand beaches, lush foliage, and a bedroom overlooking the Atlantic. Of, course we'll have to pack our things tonight, but it's a small price to pay for an entire week away alone. No book deadlines. No Schutts. No Sharon." He punctuated the statement with a mock shiver. "No Jameson. And, most of all, no murders. What do you think, darling?"

Marjorie didn't answer.

"Honey pie?" Creighton nudged her shoulder, only to receive a loud snore in response. He kissed her lightly on the forehead. "I knew you'd be excited."

The buildings lining Hamilton Harbor shimmered like a strand of pink pearls in the summer mid-Atlantic sun. Marjorie — looking well-rested and ready for fun in a belted red plaid sundress with shoulder ties — stepped onto the gangway, adjusted the brim of her floppy red hat, and wondered if she weren't the luckiest woman on earth. Lucky to be in a tropical paradise with the man she loved and even luckier to have shed the nauseating confines of their cramped

14

cruise ship stateroom.

Creighton, dapper as always in his cream-colored summer suit, slid an arm around her waist and kissed her hair. "Happy?"

She drew a deep breath and sighed. "Mmmmmm . . . very."

He smiled. "I'm glad. I spoke with the ship steward; he'll have our things sent to the house this afternoon. Until then, I thought perhaps we'd head over there, get you acquainted with the place, maybe go for a swim . . ."

Marjorie narrowed her eyes. "But my suit is packed away."

"Exactly." Creighton grinned.

"Why, Mr. Ashcroft, you're incorrigible," she purred.

"You don't know the half of it." He tilted his hat at a rakish angle and winked. "Now then, all we need to do is find the boat and we're on our way."

Marjorie felt a sudden rash of heartburn. "Boat?"

"Yes. Normally, our houseboy, George, would have met us in the speedster, but there's no telephone at the house and there wasn't sufficient time to wire ahead. So the steward contacted the harbor master and arranged for one of the locals to take us over."

"In a boat," she confirmed.

"Yes, in a boat. It's an island, darling. There's no other way of getting there." He smiled reassuringly. "Now don't worry, sweetheart, the motors on these smaller boats slice through the waves like hot butter — why, you won't feel a thing!"

THREE

Officer Patrick Noonan crouched behind the pair of metal trashcans that stood guard at the back door of the McClelland cottage. He lifted the pair of police-issued binoculars to his eyes and trained them on the hedges that lined the southern perimeter of the yard.

"Come on." He quietly urged the subject of his search to emerge from the neatly trimmed yew branches. "Come out and show yourself. I know you're in there, you coward."

As if on cue, the culprit emerged from the hedges, paused to survey his surroundings, and then inched stealthily toward the back door of the cottage.

"That's it," Noonan thought to himself. "I've got you now. I've —"

"Noonan!" boomed the deep baritone of Detective Robert Jameson from the front yard.

The subject stopped cold in his tracks before beating a hasty retreat into the darkness of the yew boughs.

Robert Jameson appeared in the driveway, his cool, dark good looks more reminiscent of a matinee idol than a government employee. "Noonan," he addressed his short, stocky counterpart. "I've been looking all over for you. What have you been doing?"

Noonan rose awkwardly from behind the trashcans. "I, uh —"

Jameson didn't give him a chance to respond. He quickly removed the binoculars from around Noonan's neck. "What are these for? Bird watching?"

The officer snatched the binoculars back, indignantly. "No, they're not for bird watching. You know I've been checking up on Marjorie's place while she and Creighton are on their honeymoon."

Jameson took Noonan squarely by the shoulders and turned him around so that he was facing the backdoor. "There. That's the house — you don't need binoculars."

"Go ahead, boss. Laugh it up," Noonan responded sarcastically.

"Okay, okay," Jameson said soothingly. "So what happened?"

"So I came by here during my lunch break today, just to check up on things and I saw

18

someone suspicious lurking around the neighborhood."

"Someone suspicious?" Jameson's eyes narrowed. "Where?"

"He was on the green when I first spotted him. Then he came up the driveway, just like you did."

"He came up the driveway? That's pretty nervy."

"Yeah," Noonan agreed. "Yeah, he's as bold as brass, this one. I followed him, but when he saw me, he took off behind the hedges."

"Those hedges?" Jameson asked as he indicated the dense line of yews at the rear of the property. "A guy would have to be pretty wiry to fit through growth that thick."

Noonan nodded. "He's a wiry little guy alright. And stealthy — like a . . . like a cat."

"Hmm. What color was his hair?"

"Ohhhh," Noonan removed his hat and scratched his head. "Gray and black and white . . ."

"Salt and pepper?" Jameson confirmed.

"For what?"

"Salt and pepper is what they call black hair with gray," Jameson explained.

"Well, it might be more like gray hair with white and a little bit of black," Noonan clarified.

"Gray hair," the Detective paraphrased. "What color eyes?"

"Yellow," Noonan answered without even thinking.

"Yellow? People don't have yellow eyes, Noonan."

"Did I say yellow? Nah, green . . . ish, with yellow bits in them."

Jameson leaned in. "How close were you to this guy? 'Greenish with yellow bits' sounds like you were . . . well . . . dancing."

"Dancing?"

Jameson laughed out loud. "I'm joking around with you, Noonan."

"You've got an awfully good sense of humor today," Noonan noted. "Did ya see your girlfriend at lunch or something?"

"What girlfriend?"

"Sharon Schutt. You know: short, chubby, thinks you're 'positively aces,' " Noonan teased in a falsetto voice.

"Sharon isn't my girlfriend," Jameson denied. "I have dinner with her and her folks every now and then."

"Every now and then?" Noonan repeated. "You're over there three, maybe four, times a week."

"Yeah, but it's not like she and I are an item or anything."

Noonan laughed. "Uh huh, keep telling

yourself that."

"We're not an item," he maintained. "When Marjorie and I were engaged, she'd cook for me five times a week. Now that she and Creighton are married . . . well . . . it's tough going without a home-cooked meal. The Schutts have been darned nice to invite me over as often as they do."

"They invite you so you'll make the goo-goo eyes at Sharon. They did it to Creighton Ashcroft, too." Noonan shook his head, "And you call yourself a detective."

"I don't like Sharon in that way," Jameson explained.

"I don't think that matters much to the Schutts. They're looking to send Sharon on the next train to 'Marriagetown,' and, you, my friend, are the express."

"I'll keep an eye out for Sharon, Noonan, so long as you keep an eye out for our suspicious character. He might be looking to rob the place." Jameson frowned. "And we wouldn't want anything to ruin Marjorie's honeymoon."

FOUR

The wooden fishing boat docked in a small, sandy cove surrounded by dark limestone cliffs. Creighton helped his bride onto the narrow pier and then dispatched the boat captain, a local man, with a silent "thank you," and a few crumpled bills.

"How's the stomach?" He shouted over the noise of the fishing boat engine and planted a loud kiss on Marjorie's cheek.

"Fine," she shouted back, "but my knees are a bit wobbly. I guess I haven't gotten my land legs back yet."

Creighton shook his head. "The sea has nothing to do with it," he yelled. "It's me; but don't worry, you'll get used to it in a year or two."

Marjorie rolled her eyes and followed her husband along the pier and up a narrow flight of wooden steps that scaled the face of the cliff. Given the weathered stairs and secluded nature of the island, Marjorie expected to be greeted by a humble cottage set amid a few lazy palm trees. The sight awaiting her at the top of the cliff couldn't have been more different.

Combining the best of both West Indian and Bermudian architecture, the pastel pink residence was imposing in size and symmetry and featured quoining and elaborate dentil moldings. Raised high on a stone foundation that was designed to act as both slave quarters and a buffer against rising flood waters, the top two stories were encircled by wide verandahs with whitewashed balustrades. Access to the home was provided by a set of twin stairs, which led to a heavy carved wooden door set beneath an exquisite fanlight; access to the verandahs was provided by floor-to-ceiling windows accented by dark green shutters.

Marjorie stood on the gravel path that bisected the acres of well-manicured lawn and stared, slack-jawed, at her new accommodations.

"Welcome to *Ilha Negra*," Creighton announced happily. "Well, *Black Island*, actually; named after the dark limestone cliffs we saw down at the cove. My mother thought the name too dark and ominous — in truth, she thought the English language and its hard consonants to be quite unromantic. So, after speaking with some of the Portuguese residents in Hamilton, she translated it *Ilha Negra* and petitioned to have it named such on all the maps."

"Did she succeed?" Marjorie inquired.

Creighton shook his head. "No. I thought she stood a good chance. After all, Bermuda used to be called the 'Isle of Devils' — a name, I imagine, that had more to do with rum than storms. The local magistrates, however, vetoed my mother's idea; apparently the name 'Bermuda' provided the local population with all the romance they could ever require, thank you very much." He took her hand and pulled her along the gravel. "But enough talk about history. I'll introduce you to Selina and George and then we can go make some history of our own."

Marjorie followed Creighton across the expansive lawn and around the back of the house. Here, the path split into three: one route led to a small potting shed, another to the stables, and the last to a small cottage bearing the same pink paint, tall windows, and green shutters as the main house.

Creighton guided Marjorie to the cottage and knocked upon the bottom half of the partially open Dutch door. Inside the cottage, Marjorie could make out the shape of a woman standing over a stove.

"What is it, George?" she asked in a strong Bermudian accent. "Can't you see my hands are dirty?" she chided as she turned around. At the sight of Creighton, she gasped.

"Hullo, Selina," the Englishman grinned. "Is that the warm welcome I get after all these years?"

Selina, dressed in a bright yellow house-dress and a matching headscarf, was a tall, dark-skinned, slender woman in her early fifties. Her face, although lined with creases of care and hard work, was extremely handsome. In her youth, Selina must have been admired island-wide for her beauty.

Selina laughed and wiped her hands on her apron before throwing her arms around Creighton's neck. "Oh, Mr. Creighton! It's so good to see you. No one told me you were coming —"

"We didn't know either. We just 'happened' to be in the neighborhood."

"In the neighborhood!" Selina stepped back and waved a chiding finger. "Why, Mr. Creighton, you haven't changed a bit. You've still got the devil in you! Why you drove —" She caught a glimpse of Marjorie and smiled and bowed self-consciously. "Oh, I'm sorry, Miss. I was so surprised by Mr.

Creighton, I did not see you there. You must be a friend of Mr. Creighton."

"She's a little more than that, Selina," Creighton advised. "She's my wife."

"Your . . . ? Oh my goodness! You got married?! When?"

"A few days ago. We're on our honeymoon." He slid his arm around Marjorie's waist and drew her to him. "Selina Pooley, meet Marjorie McClelland Ashcroft."

Marjorie extended her hand. "Pleased to meet you."

"A pleasure to meet you too, Ma'am." Selina grasped it warmly and then began to chuckle. "Married? Oh, I need to tell George! He will never believe it!"

She excused herself and scurried through the open Dutch door and down the path to the stables. "George!" she called. "George! Come here!"

Marjorie's eyes slid surreptitiously toward Creighton. "So, you've brought a few 'friends' here, have you?"

Creighton's face colored slightly. "Oh, a party or two back during Prohibition. Silly kid stuff. You know how boys are . . ."

"Indeed," Marjorie concurred with a sly grin.

Selina returned with her son, George, close at her heels. "Look who it is, George!"

she exclaimed.

Eighteen-year-old George Pooley was tall, muscular, and lighter skinned than his mother. But the most striking feature of this handsome young man was his blue-gray eyes; an unusual characteristic, Marjorie noted, for a person of African descent.

"Mr. Creighton!" George greeted enthusiastically, as he shook Creighton's hand.

Creighton did a double take. "George? Good Lord, what have you been eating? The last time I saw you, you were this high." Creighton extricated his hand from George's strong grip and raised it to the center of his chest.

"That's because last time you saw George, he was still in school," Selina explained.

"You're out of school already?" Creighton repeated in disbelief.

George smiled and nodded. "Last month."

"Graduated at the top of his class," Selina added proudly.

"Top? That's terrific, George," Creighton remarked.

"Thank you," the young man replied uncomfortably. "Mother told me that you had good news as well. What is it?"

"I am now a married man." Creighton took Marjorie by the wrist and pulled her beside him. "Meet the new Mrs. Ashcroft.

George, this is Marjorie; Marjorie, this is Selina's son, George."

"Yes, I got that much," Marjorie laughed as she extended her hand. "How do you do, George?"

George took her hand in both of his. "A pleasure, Ma'am. Congratulations to you both. Although this isn't the first time we've met. You came with Mr. Creighton last time he was here. Except back then your hair was red."

"I — I've never been here," Marjorie said haltingly.

George's eyes grew wide as Creighton drew a finger across his throat.

"Oh . . . I'm sorry, Ma'am. I'm mistaken." George apologized, and then quickly added: "I must have been thinking of someone else."

"Yes," Creighton chimed in with a nervous laugh. "You're thinking of my brother, Edward. I believe he was seeing a redhead before he married Prudence. Wasn't he, Selina?"

"Yes, I think he did," Selina played along.

"So, George," Creighton segued to a new subject, "now that you're out of school, what are your plans?"

"Your father offered me a job here," George replied. "Managing the property."

"That's all well and good. But is that what you want to do?" Creighton pressed. "You graduated at the top of your class; the world is your oyster."

"I would like to continue my studies," the young man confessed.

"Then you should. There are plenty of wonderful schools in the States that would accept you."

"We have no way to pay for that," Selina explained.

"Yes, you do," Creighton argued. "My father's known you, Selina, since he and my mother married, and he's known George since he was a baby. It doesn't seem unreasonable to ask him for the money to send George to school."

"I already did," Selina frowned. "He said, 'no.' "

"Figures," Creighton smirked. "It's in the old man's best interest to keep George here. However, I'm not giving up that easily. As soon as I get home, I'll give dear old Dad a call and see what I can do."

George's and Selina's faces were a question.

"*Call* your father?" they repeated in unison.

"Child, you don't need to call him," Selina continued. "He's here!"

FIVE

"He's here?" Marjorie echoed in disbelief.

"You're joking," Creighton insisted.

"I am serious!" Selina became indignant. "He arrived yesterday. I thought that was why you were here — to tell him of your marriage. I thought you knew."

"No, I didn't know. How could I? It's not March; it's August. He's never here in August."

"It is unusual," Selina agreed. "When he telegrammed last week to tell me to prepare the house, I was very surprised. Your father likes his habits. But things change and people change. I figure his new wife was tired of the city and wanted a holiday."

Creighton reared back "New wife? Father's remarried?"

"Yes, a few months ago. She appears to be much younger than he is."

"Humph, naturally. Well, I suppose it could be worse; he could still be seeing that wretched secretary of his."

"Oh no, your father has a new secretary, a man by the name of Miller."

"You've met him?"

"Yes, he's here at the house." George stated.

Creighton removed his hat and scratched his head. "That's odd. Father's the frugal type. He wouldn't pay to bring his secretary along on holiday unless he had business to conduct. In the past, it was monkey business, but now . . ."

"It struck me as strange, too," Selina admitted. "Do you know of any business your father might be doing here in Bermuda?"

Creighton placed his hat back onto his head and shrugged. "No, but that's none of my concern any longer." He offered his arm to Marjorie, who happily accepted, and made his way toward the door. "Selina. George. It was wonderful seeing you both again, but if you'll excuse us, Marjorie and I have a honeymoon to conduct."

"Where are you going?" Selina inquired as she blocked their path.

"Hamilton. To find a hotel."

"What about your father?"

"Tell him I said congratulations on his

marriage and on finally getting rid of Griselda."

"Who?"

"My father's former secretary."

Selina's eyebrows furrowed. "His secretary was named Griselda, too?"

Creighton's mouth formed a tiny 'O'. "Too? You mean that . . . oh . . . oh no . . . oh no . . . my father married Griselda. That's why he suddenly has a male secretary. Oh, no. Oh, brother."

"Yes, your brother is here," George stated. "And Miss Prudence also."

"And Miss Prudence's friend," Selina added. "A woman named Cassandra; she says she can talk to spirits."

Creighton broke into maniacal laughter.

"Are you all right?" Marjorie asked in alarm.

"I'm fine, darling," Creighton reassured as he settled down. "Simply laughing at the irony of it all: we elope to avoid a carnival of a wedding only to wind up at a circus of a family reunion."

" 'Wind up?' " Selina repeated hopefully. "Does that mean you're staying?"

"No, it does not. Although I admire your optimism." Creighton gave Selina a quick kiss on the cheek and pushed her gently out of the way. "I'll give you the name of our hotel so that you and George can meet us for dinner one evening," he added as he opened the bottom half of the Dutch door and stepped into the hot Bermuda sun.

From there, Creighton and Marjorie hastened back to the cove and the speedster, which was at its spot at the pier. The sight of the tiny boat and the promise of his and Marjorie's imminent escape from Black Island was enough to make Creighton shout in excitement.

And shout he nearly did — until he noticed a figure farther up the path, heading in their direction.

Six

Griselda Ridgley Ashcroft was a marvel of 1930s beauty science. Her Benzedrine-thin body was tinted a bright orange through a generous application of dihydroxyacetone, and her peroxide blonde permanent-waved hair blew in the breeze. She reached a Bakelite-bangled arm toward her derrière, adjusted the seat of her provacative maillot swimsuit, and teetered toward Creighton on a pair of high-heeled gold lamé sandals.

"Creighton," Griselda cried before leaving a lip-shaped stain of bright red beeswax and castor oil upon Creighton's face. She turned around and shouted down to the cliff-side staircase. "Baby! Baby, guess who's here!"

The intimidating form of Creighton Richard Ashcroft II emerged at the top of the stairs. Marjorie immediately noticed that the younger Ashcroft bore little resemblance to his father. Whereas Creighton's hair was a warm, rich shade of chestnut, his father's

34

was a stark jet black with undertones of cool blue. While Creighton was tall, finely boned, and elegantly proportioned, the senior Ashcroft — albeit of equal height — was somewhat top-heavy and thick-bodied. And whereas Creighton's face could be described as classically handsome and refined, the elder Ashcroft appeared boorish and menacing.

Even their eyes, both blue, were of different hues: Creighton II's were an icy shade of near gray; Creighton III's a pure, deep azure.

"Hullo, Dad," Creighton greeted.

The elder Ashcroft glared as he smoothed the hem of his cream-colored nautically-inspired blazer, then thrust his hands into the pockets of his navy blue trousers. "The prodigal son returns, eh?" he remarked in a Cockney accent. "I was waiting for this day; the day you'd run out of money and come back to me. So, what is it that you want?"

Creighton sighed deeply and shook his head. "Want? I don't want anything except for you to get out of my way." He shoved past his father and headed toward the stairs.

Marjorie followed her husband, eager to escape the feeling of foreboding she had experienced since she had arrived on the island.

"Wait!" Mr. Ashcroft commanded.

Creighton halted, his foot hovering over the top step.

"If you didn't come for money, why are you here?"

The younger Ashcroft slowly turned around and drew a deep breath before answering, "I'm — we're — on our honeymoon."

"Finally married, eh?" Mr. Ashcroft scoffed. "High time. Considering all the society girls I had you introduced to, you'd think you'd have done it sooner. But, no, not Creighton. No, to him, they were too old or too young, too short or too tall, too serious or too frivolous. The list went on and on . . ."

Griselda tittered briefly and then went back to examining her Chinese red-lacquered fingernails, each one perfectly polished to leave the moon and tip bare.

Mr. Ashcroft scratched his chin and gave his new daughter-in-law the once-over. "So, this is what you chose when left to your own devices."

"With all due respect, sir, I'm not a 'what,' I'm a 'whom.' " Marjorie extended her hand, "Marjorie McClelland — I mean, Ashcroft. I keep forgetting . . . but then again, it's only been four days."

36

Mr. Ashcroft accepted the hand and gave it a tepid squeeze before letting it drop. "Well, she's pretty enough," he deemed aloud.

At the word "pretty," Griselda looked up from her fingernails and shot her husband a dirty look.

"But does she have a brain in her head?" the older man continued.

"Of course," Creighton replied.

"And all my teeth, too," Marjorie added sotto voce.

Creighton gave her a pinch on the rump.

"Ow!" she shouted.

"Marjorie's a writer, Father," Creighton offered. "She's written four —"

"Five," Marjorie corrected.

"Sorry. Five mystery novels to date, as well as a true crime book in the works. She's also solved a few mysteries in her day, using not much more than observation and intuition."

Mr. Ashcroft gave a quiet, approving nod. After a prolonged pause, he announced, "Drinks will be at seven-thirty this evening, followed by dinner at eight. Sharp."

Creighton shook his head. "You don't understand, Father. We're not staying here."

The elder Ashcroft shrugged. "Suit yourself. I don't care. But if you're looking for a hotel, I doubt you'll find one. The regatta starts this weekend; all of Hamilton is booked."

Creighton removed his hat and ran a hand through his chestnut hair.

"However, you are having dinner with us tonight. I'm sure you didn't have a proper wedding —"

"The ship's captain did an adequate job," Marjorie tried to interject.

"The least you can do is have a proper celebration dinner," Mr. Ashcroft chided over his daughter-in-law's argument. "A toast to your marriage and all that nonsense. While we're at it, you can toast Griselda and me as well." He placed an arm about his wife's shoulders.

As if on cue, she thrust her left hand in front of Marjorie's face to display a gaudy, oversized sapphire and diamond ring.

"That's lovely," Marjorie stated politely, once her eyes had adjusted focus.

"Yes, Selina told me the news," Creighton said matter-of-factly. "Congratulations, Father." He turned his attention to his new stepmother. "Congratulations, *Grizz*. Or shall I call you 'Mum'?"

"Why you —" Griselda started in a nasal New Jersey tone, but quickly checked herself. " 'Grizz' is fine," she mustered with a pseudo-English accent that was more Margaret Dumont than Lady Windsor. "I'd better tell Selina to expect two more for dinner." She excused herself and tottered off to the house.

Mr. Ashcroft tipped his Captain's hat before heading up the trail after his wife. "Seven-thirty, sharp," he reminded his son. "Marjorie, I look forward to discussing your occupation in more depth. I'd like to get your professional opinion on some matters."

When he was out of earshot, Marjorie turned to Creighton. "I don't know much about your father, but he doesn't seem that bad to me. A little rough around the edges, maybe . . ."

Creighton pulled a face. "He's on his best behavior."

"Well, he just met me. Maybe he wants to make a good impression," Marjorie suggested.

"No, he's up to something."

"Up to something? Like what?"

"I don't know, darling. But we'd both best be careful."

SEVEN

Marjorie and Creighton returned from their trip to Hamilton, as Mr. Ashcroft predicted, without a hotel room. However, their trip had produced a collection of boxes in a dizzying array of sizes, colors, and shapes.

"I'm so glad we got some clothing that didn't come from the ship's boutique," Marjorie remarked as they scaled the front steps of the Black Island mansion. "I was starting to feel like an advertisement for White Star Lines."

"Well, next time we elope immediately after solving a murder case on a ship, I'll make sure we pack first, darling."

"Although it could have been worse. If the ship purser hadn't allowed us to use Michael Barnwell and Veronica Carter's stateroom, we might have spent our wedding night in a broom closet or a lifeboat."

"Now that would have been a story for the grandchildren," Creighton quipped from behind the stack of boxes he was balancing in his arms. "Can you open the door for me, dear?"

Marjorie complied and the couple stepped into the front hall of the residence. With whitewashed walls, a hand-blown glass hanging lantern, and a Bermuda chest with cabriole legs, the room was minimally furnished, creating an atmosphere of cool comfort.

Creighton led the way up the massive portrait-lined cedar staircase, down the hall, and into the second room on the right. "Here we are," he announced as he dropped the parcels on the canopied four-poster bed.

In addition to the intricately carved bed, the southwest-corner bedroom contained a Sheraton mahogany four-drawer chest, two silk upholstered wing chairs, and a rosewood bedside table. However, the stars of the room were the floor-to-ceiling windows that lined the two far, perpendicular walls. They overlooked a wide expanse of ocean punctuated by small dots of land.

Marjorie gasped in delight as she stepped through a window and out onto the verandah. Up here, above the trees and dense vegetation, the clean ocean air circulated freely. It provided a breezy refuge for the island's human inhabitants and a cool napping spot for the small, fluffy black cat curled up on the verandah floor just outside Marjorie and Creighton's bedroom.

Creighton followed his wife through the window and smiled as he watched her stoop down and scratch the stray behind the ears.

"How's that?" she asked the young cat as he purred and rolled onto his back. "Does that feel good?"

"You know, I'll roll around like that too if you rub me the right way," Creighton remarked with a twinkle in his eye.

Marjorie stood up and threw her arms around her husband's neck. "Hmmm. That, I'd like to see."

"Coming right up," Creighton quipped as he wrapped his arms around her waist and kissed her.

All the while, the scrawny black cat meowed and rubbed against Marjorie's leg.

"I know this honeymoon hasn't been a lot of fun for you," Creighton acknowledged. "Between your seasickness and then finding my whole family here —"

"I don't mind your family being here," Marjorie said supportively as she reached down and picked up the mewing cat. "I won't lie and say it wouldn't have been nicer had we been alone, but I want to get to know your family. I want to know everything about you."

She gazed out upon the water and the low-hanging red sun. "I couldn't imagine a more beautiful place to be right now."

"I couldn't imagine a more beautiful woman to be with," Creighton replied as he undid the shoulder tie of her sundress and kissed her again.

Marjorie kissed him back and then, opening one eye, glanced at her watch. "Oh!" she cried. "Drinks are at seven-thirty. We only have —"

Creighton drowned out her next words by placing his mouth on hers. "We have time enough," he reassured as he pulled her back through the bedroom window.

Moments later, Creighton could be seen closing the shutters of the bedroom. But not before evicting a certain black cat.

EIGHT

Giggling and snorting, Marjorie and Creighton stumbled down the large cedar staircase just as the grandfather clock in the study sounded the half hour.

Upon reaching the entry hall, they exchanged a quick kiss and re-examined each other's appearance for any evidence of their recent activities. Perhaps it was the glow of love, but they could find few flaws. Creighton was dashing in his recently purchased white dinner jacket with silk piping, black tie, and black trousers, and Marjorie resplendent in a new green silk t-back evening gown, silver pumps, and a pair of emerald and diamond earrings. After a quick straightening of Creighton's tie by Marjorie and an even quicker pat of Marjorie's bottom by Creighton, they walked, arm-in-arm, into the study to face the Ashcroft family.

Fitted with cedar bookshelves, an Adams-style fireplace, and satin drapes in a classic palm frond motif, the study made an intimate gathering area for hors d'oeuvres and aperitifs.

Griselda had changed from her swimsuit into a retina-damaging gold-sequined evening gown with a daringly low back. She played the role of hostess to the hilt. "Manhattans?" she asked Marjorie and Creighton as she leaned over the well-stocked bar trolley.

They nodded their consent and were immediately accosted by a small, slightly plump woman in a black, ruffle-sleeved evening dress that overwhelmed her small stature.

"Creighton!" she exclaimed in a soft English accent, as she endeavored to stretch her short arms around Creighton's tall frame.

"Hi, Pru. It's wonderful to see you," Creighton greeted, as he leaned down and planted a kiss on his sister-in-law's cheek.

"And I know who this is," she asserted as she moved to Creighton's wife. "You must be Marjorie! I'm Prudence, but you can call me Pru. I'm so glad we're going to be sisters. It's been just me and the men for much too long."

Griselda handed a couple of Manhattans to Creighton and Marjorie before mocking

45

Pru. "*It's been just me and the men for much too long.* Who do I look like? Tommy Dorsey?"

"No," Creighton quipped, "but in that dress, you could pass as his trombone."

Griselda bared her teeth at Creighton and went back to her bartending duties.

Marjorie, holding her drink in one hand, leaned down and hugged her sister-in-law with the other. "I'm glad we're going to be sisters, too."

It was a true statement. Whether it was because of the woman's sweet, gentle face or the complete ingenuousness of her words and actions, Marjorie took an instant liking to Pru. Unfortunately, she also sensed that Pru might be the sort of soul who required protection from the less-than-kind characters in the world.

This suspicion was borne out as Pru summoned a woman from across the room. She was dressed in a white, floor-length tunic with bell sleeves that set off her dark olive complexion; her straight black hair was pulled into a tight chignon, and around her neck she wore a large gold pendant fashioned in the Egyptian style.

"I want you both to meet someone. Cassandra, this is my brother-in-law, Creighton," Pru introduced.

"How do you do?" Creighton asked as he extended his hand.

Cassandra did not accept it, but stood, palms together, as if in prayer.

"And this," Pru went on, "is Creighton's wife — my new sister-in-law, Marjorie."

Marjorie did her best to mimic Cassandra's pose while simultaneously juggling her cocktail glass. She then punctuated the pose with a small bow.

Again, Cassandra was motionless.

"Cassandra is a spiritualist and medium," Pru announced. "She's been helping me get in touch with my spirit guide, Omari."

"Ahhhh," Marjorie and Creighton sang in unison.

"Prudence's guide is tall, strong, and handsome; he stands at her right side, as he has done since her birth many ages ago in ancient Egypt," Cassandra explained.

"Isn't she wonderful?" Pru exclaimed. "Cassandra has helped me understand my purpose. Before I met her, I felt so bored . . . so unfulfilled. Edward and I still live with Father, so we have no home of our own. No children. Cassandra made me understand that I am paying debts from my past life, but that I am not alone. Omari is with me, helping me along."

"That's — that's wonderful," Marjorie

politely remarked.

Creighton, however, would not leave well enough alone. "You mean to say," he started, "that we all have these spiritual guides?"

"Yes," Cassandra confirmed.

"Then Marjorie and I have them, too?"

"Indeed."

"Well, don't hold back," Creighton prompted. "Tell us about our guides."

Cassandra stared at Marjorie for several seconds. "You, fair lady, are smiled upon by the most powerful and sacred, Bastet. The goddess Bastet is the protector of all women, children and felines, but with you, her presence is especially strong."

"How lovely. Thank you." Marjorie smiled broadly and took a sip of her Manhattan.

As Creighton broke into uproarious laughter, a man joined them. He was similar in height and build to Creighton, but his coloring and facial features were the spitting image of the elder Ashcroft.

"What's going on?" he asked.

"Hullo, Edward," Creighton greeted him. "I don't think you've met my wife, Marjorie."

"No I haven't, but she was all Father talked about this afternoon." Edward extended his hand in welcome. "Welcome to the family, Marjorie."

Marjorie accepted his hand and smiled graciously.

"Cassandra was just telling us that Marjorie is the favorite of the Egyptian goddess, Bastet," Creighton explained to his brother.

"What's wrong with that?" Marjorie demanded.

"Nothing," Creighton allowed, "except that we'll need two staterooms for the trip home: one for me and the other for that swollen head of yours."

"Ha, ha," Marjorie responded in mock laughter. "Why don't we find out about your guide?"

"All right," Creighton agreed. "Go ahead, Cassandra. Is it an Egyptian god, or better yet, a gorgeous, scantily clad Egyptian goddess?"

Marjorie gave him a playful punch in the arm.

"Your guide is Basenji," Cassandra coolly stated.

"Basenji," Creighton slowly repeated. "Is that a male or a female?"

"Neither. It is a barkless Egyptian dog." With that, Cassandra turned on one heel and retreated from the study.

"Oh, you've done it now. She's terrible when she's angry." Pru took off after her instructor.

"How do you feel about that whole thing?" Creighton prodded his brother after Pru had left the room.

"What whole thing?" Edward replied obtusely. "Oh, you mean Cassandra? It's all a bunch of nonsense. Spirit guides, bah!"

"I know that, but Cassandra's being paid for that nonsense, isn't she?"

"Oh yes, and handsomely too."

"And you don't mind paying an obvious fraud?"

"Not if it makes Pru happy." Edward shook his head. "You don't know what it was like before Cassandra came along. Pru was constantly talking about getting our own house and starting a family."

"Well, how long have you been married now? Five years? Those seem like reasonable things for a woman in her position to want," Creighton asserted as he glanced at Marjorie.

Marjorie, polishing off her drink, nodded in agreement.

"And she shall have them once Father is gone," Edward maintained. "But right now, I'm somewhat tied to the old man's purse strings."

A bell sounded and the party shuffled out

of the study and into the adjacent dining room.

Beneath the candlelight of an intricately carved Waterford chandelier, Creighton Ashcroft II took his place at the head of the heavy British Colonial table and beckoned his guests to be seated.

Opposite Mr. Ashcroft, at the other end of the table, sat Griselda. To his right sat Prudence, Creighton, and Cassandra. To his left sat Edward and Marjorie. An empty chair occupied the spot between Marjorie and Griselda and opposite Cassandra.

George entered the room through a paneled door and began pouring the wine.

"Thank you, George." Mr. Ashcroft grabbed his wine glass and rose from his chair. "And thank you, everyone, for being here this evening. As you know —"

The paneled door once again swung open, this time admitting to a bespectacled man of slight build and thinning hair. He fiddled nervously with the lapels of his drape-cut suit as he scurried to his seat.

"You're late, Miller," Ashcroft admonished.

Miller pushed his spectacles farther up the bridge of his nose. "I'm sorry," he murmured.

Ashcroft gave a loud sigh of exasperation.

51

"As I was saying, tonight is a night of celebration. After having met every debutante in New York and London, after enjoying dinner and brandy with all the well-propertied spinsters in our social circle, and even having dallied with a few dancers from the Ziegfeld Follies —"

Marjorie shot a look at her husband, who merely smiled and shrugged.

"— my eldest son, Creighton, has finally found himself a bride. And what a lovely bride she is. Please join me as I toast to Creighton and Marjorie's happiness. May they enjoy a long, happy life together."

"Here, here," Edward rejoined before they all completed the toast with a hearty sip.

"Since no wedding would be complete without a gift," Ashcroft continued, "I would like to take this opportunity to present them with something I know Creighton's mother would have wanted them to have." He nodded to George who, after serving the wine, stood waiting in a dark corner of the room.

George obediently walked over to what initially appeared to be a low, covered buffet table and pulled back the cloth to reveal a carved walnut Italian Renaissance chest.

"The cassone Mother bought in Italy," Creighton said in disbelief. "I didn't realize you still had it. Where was it?"

"It's been here the whole time. Packed away," Ashcroft explained.

Creighton felt a lump form in his throat. "I don't know what to say. Thank you."

"Yes, thank you," Marjorie echoed.

Ashcroft waved his hand dismissively. "And now that the formalities are out of the way, I have a personal announcement I'd like to make. George, could you bring your mother in here, please?"

As George retrieved Selina from the kitchen, Mr. Ashcroft's audience exchanged questioning glances, each person looking to the other for some indication of what was to come next.

Once Selina was seated by the kitchen door, Mr. Ashcroft cleared his throat. "As you all may, or may not, know, last month marked my sixty-fifth year on this earth. Being closer in years to his death than his birth makes a man reassess his life. It was during the process of reassessing my life that I came to an eye-opening, somewhat disappointing conclusion: that none of you are worth my time, my energy, or, most importantly, my money."

There was a loud uproar from his audience, but Ashcroft quelled their murmurs, gasps, and protests, with a raise of his hand.

53

"You have all been written out of my will."

Another uproar followed. This time, Ashcroft let it die out on its own. "You are all out of my will," he repeated, "except for one worthy individual."

His audience, once again, exchanged puzzled glances.

"Selina, my loyal employee for nearly thirty years now," Ashcroft started amid murmurs and whispers. "Yesterday, you asked me for the money to send your beloved son to university. When I refused, you threatened to blackmail me."

"I was out of my head," Selina explained. "I was angry . . . I —"

"Whatever your reasons, I will beat you to the punch," Ashcroft trumped. "George is my son."

The news produced a series of horrified gasps from his audience — with the exclusion of Marjorie who stared open-mouthed at her dining companions. "Are you joking? No one here guessed that Mr. Ashcroft was George's father? They have the same eyes! It gave me pause once or twice — and I only just arrived this morning." Realizing her faux pas, she drew her hand to her mouth. "Sorry . . . I . . . go on."

George, meanwhile, was fuming. "Is it true, mother?" he asked.

Selina nodded.

"Why didn't you tell me? And you," George pointed at his father, "you knew I was your son, but you kept me here as an indentured servant. I hate you!!"

"So do my other sons. Why should you be any different?" Ashcroft remarked before turning his attention to the opposite end of the table.

"Griselda, my darling wife," he started.

"Yes, sweetheart," she replied in a saccharine tone.

"You were my secretary long before you were ever my wife. As such, I thought I could trust you."

"You can," she assured.

"Can I? I've taken a look at your spending over the past few months. The generous allowance I give you hasn't been spent entirely on dresses, hats, or hairdressing. You've spent some of it on those things, grant you, but the rest of it has been used to pay the rent on a small flat in northern New Jersey."

"But —" she began to argue.

"I can only imagine what you do there and with whom," he stated.

"I wouldn't," Griselda cried, sending a cascade of black mascara down her face. "I swear I wouldn't!"

Cassandra reached over and placed a

comforting hand on Griselda's shoulder. "Do not despair; your spirit guide will not let you fall."

Mr. Ashcroft started laughing uncontrollably. "You may want to consult your 'spirit guide' in a moment, Cassandra. Or shall I call you Rose? That's your real name, isn't it? Your last position as a spiritual 'teacher' was in Rhode Island, and it resulted in your being named as the sole beneficiary of an old lady's will. When the woman met with an unfortunate 'accident' and you inherited the entire fortune, the family contested the will and ran you out of town."

"Father!" Prudence exclaimed. "How can you say such a horrible thing about Cassandra? She's my friend . . . she has a gift!"

Marjorie leapt from her chair and ran to the other side of the table. Taking a weeping Prudence into her arms, she shouted, "How can you be so kind and then be so cruel? Don't you know, Mr. Ashcroft . . . ? Don't you realize?" her voice trailed off.

"I know," he replied. "I know that Prudence is craving what her husband can't, or isn't, willing to give her."

Edward rose from his seat. "That's enough, Father."

"You've lingered for years, under the pretense of being the 'diligent' son. Living at the family home, working at the company, but what you were really hanging on to was the hope of your inheritance. Meanwhile, your wife was withering away from loneliness. Of course, a better woman would have told her husband to quit years ago."

"Mr. Ashcroft, sir," Miller spoke in a tremulous voice. "Edward is in charge of . . . I wouldn't . . ."

"Mr. Miller," Ashcroft addressed his secretary, "you've already wasted my time with that sham of an appointment and by arriving late to dinner. You are in no position to advise me of what to do. In fact, you're in no position at all. You're fired."

Miller stood up and scurried from the dining room in a fashion reminiscent of his entrance.

In the meantime, Edward had picked up his wine glass and sent it shattering against the wall behind his father. "Damn you!" he shouted as he made his exit. "Damn you!"

As Miller and Edward made their dramatic departures, Creighton rose from his seat, withdrew the handkerchief from the pocket of his dinner jacket, and passed it to Marjorie, who used it to dab the tears of a sobbing Prudence.

"The only reason I agreed to this dinner was because part of me hoped that things could be different. I hoped that my marriage might start a new chapter between us. I hoped that you had changed; I knew I had. But you haven't changed at all. Despite the years, you haven't changed, have you, Father?" Creighton calmly noted. "The only joy you've ever found in this world was in building people up and then dashing their hopes. Humans, and their emotions, are nothing but playthings to you. From the time we were young, you pitted Edward and me against each other. Edward was strong, like you; I was weak like mother. Mother . . ." He said in a half-whisper as he clutched his dinner knife. "You sapped every ounce of life and happiness out of that woman. Then, after you had killed her, you pitted her children against each other in some sickening battle for your affection. You bastard! I was a fool to think you'd ever change, you —"

Selina stepped forward and took hold of both of Creighton's arms. She quietly shook her head and cautioned, "Don't do it, Mr. Creighton. Don't do it, child. You have a new wife and the whole world in front of you."

Creighton put his arms down at his sides and dropped the knife. "But Marjorie . . ." he whispered.

"Marjorie isn't going nowhere," Selina said reassuringly. "You go outside now and get some air."

With Creighton's departure, the rest of the family scattered to their quarters, leaving only Marjorie, Selina, and Mr. Ashcroft in the candle-lit dining room.

Selina took tight hold of Marjorie's hand before retreating into the kitchen. "You go to your husband," she whispered. "I'll take care of the old man."

Marjorie nodded and attempted to follow her husband, but before she could leave, Mr. Ashcroft summoned her attention. "What are your thoughts, Miss McClelland?"

He drew a piece of paper from his inside jacket pocket, unfolded it, and placed it on the table before him. Upon it, in typewritten letters, were the words: THE DAY OF RECKONING IS NIGH.

"What is this?" she asked as she picked it up.

"Someone left it on my desk yesterday evening," he explained. "I have no idea who did it, but it had to have been someone here on the island."

"And the typing?"

"Done on the typewriter on my desk. I checked the ribbon."

"More than a bit ominous." She handed the paper back to her father-in-law. "Did you call the police?"

Ashcroft refolded the paper and put in his pocket. "What could the police tell me that I don't already know? Besides, I preferred to handle this matter on my own. So I went into town this morning and had a new will drawn up, naming Creighton as the sole inheritor of my estate."

"Creighton? But —"

"He wasn't here yesterday evening. He couldn't have left the note," Ashcroft explained. "It seemed the logical next step."

"So that's what this whole dog and pony show was all about," Marjorie concluded. "This note?"

"Well, trying to prevent the writer of the note from taking any drastic action. Yes."

"And that's all?" she challenged.

"What else?"

"Pleasure," Marjorie stated bluntly. "Creighton is right; you seem to enjoy having control over other people. You enjoy having the money and power to alter their lives. The new will and your performance this evening is just another way for you to pull the strings and watch them dance. The problem is that the writer of that note isn't looking for money or anything else you can give them; they're looking to take control."

She folded her arms across her chest and shook her head slowly. "You're a master puppeteer, Mr. Ashcroft; you probably always have been. But I think . . . I think you may be in over your head this time."

"You know what, Mrs. Ashcroft?"

The use of her new surname gave Marjorie pause.

Mr. Ashcroft sunk into his high-back chair and drank back the rest of his wine. "I think I am, too."

NINE

Marjorie, her heart racing and her mind thinking only of Creighton, left the dining room. She hurried out the back door of the house and down the white gravel path. Reaching the spot where the path divided, she checked the potting shed, the stables, Selina's cottage, and their surrounding properties. There was not a soul to be seen.

She threw her hands in the air in exasperation and stopped to catch her breath. Where was Creighton? And where, for that matter, was everyone else? The scene in the dining room had caused the inhabitants of the house to scatter and disappear into the woodwork.

Marjorie retraced her steps back to the house. On a whim, she poked her head into the kitchen and then the dining room; like the cottage and stables, they, were unoccupied. Wondering if her fellow guests had retired to their rooms for the night, she proceeded down the entry hall and up the cedar staircase. As she passed the bedroom next to hers and Creighton's, she could hear, through the closed door, the slightly muffled, high-pitched voice of Prudence Ashcroft.

"I can't bear it any longer. I want him out of our lives forever!"

"I'll take care of him," Edward assured. "I promise, I'll take care of him."

"You'd better," Prudence warned. "Because if you don't do something about him, I will!"

Marjorie tiptoed quickly past the closed door and into her own bedroom. Once there, she scanned the area, and the adjoining bathroom, for any trace of her husband. She found none. She was about to head back downstairs when a cool breeze across her shoulders gave her pause.

Turning on one heel, she rushed to the windows, pushed back the shutters, and leaned outside. There, in the glow of the full moon, she could pick out a figure in white standing at the other end of the verandah. It was not Creighton's white dinner jacket reflecting the moonlight, but Cassandra's dress.

Marjorie watched silently as the spiritualist released her dark hair from the confines of its tight chignon, gave her head a quick shake, and took a long drag from the cigarette she was holding. As she rested her arms upon the verandah railing and exhaled a puff of smoke into the warm evening air, the small black cat that Marjorie had befriended earlier watched intently from a location midway between the two women.

Sniffing the ground as he walked, he moved closer to the woman in white, eventually coming to rest at her feet. With a loud "meow" he rubbed his head against Cassandra's bare ankle and then looked up at the woman for approval.

Cassandra gave the cat a swift kick that sent the animal airborne. He landed, feet first, about a yard away from Marjorie.

After a few moments, the cat licked his front paws, mewed slightly, and scrambled into Marjorie's waiting arms.

Her feline friend in tow, Marjorie hastened out of the bedroom, through the upstairs hallway, and down the cedar staircase. Except for the light streaming from beneath the door of the downstairs office, the sunset had left the entry hall completely dark.

Marjorie walked toward the light and gave a light rap on the door.

"Yes?" Mr. Miller replied ia a quavering voice.

Marjorie swung the door open and peeked her head inside. "I'm sorry to disturb you, Mr. Miller, especially since . . ."

"That's all right," Miller excused with an outstretched hand. "I don't think we were formally introduced. You're Marjorie, are you?"

"Yes, I am," she shook his hand warmly. "Marjorie McClelland — I mean Ashcroft."

"Miller. Herman Miller."

"You're American," Marjorie noted.

"Yes. Pennsylvania. Why?"

"Oh, I don't know, but for some reason I assumed you were English. Perhaps because the other men are," she theorized. "You know the saying: birds of a feather."

"Careful with the bird talk," he nodded at the cat. "Who's your friend?"

"Oh, he's a stray. I found him sleeping outside on the verandah."

"Lots of strays around here. Well, on the main island, at least. The place is known for them. Although I'm not certain how 'stray' they are, since they'll eat right out of your hands." He scratched the cat behind the ears. "Or stay in your arms."

"I'm sorry you lost your job," Marjorie said sympathetically.

"That's life," Miller shrugged as he stuffed a letter into an envelope. "I'm just glad I kept my references up to date. My résumé," he announced as he held the final product up for inspection.

"Good luck," Marjorie wished. "Say, did you happen to see my husband pass by here? I've been looking for him."

"I haven't seen anyone, sorry. I hope you find him though," Miller added. "He seemed very upset."

"Thanks," Marjorie said appreciatively. "He was upset. Very upset indeed."

With that, she backed out of the office door and into the hallway. She swung open the heavy front door and stepped outside, nearly falling over Griselda as she did so. The cat, jostled from Marjorie's arms, took off across the lawn.

"Oh!" Marjorie exclaimed. "Griselda, I didn't see you!"

Griselda, sobbing, was seated on the steps. In one hand, she clasped the handle of a small overnight bag; in the other, a crumpled handkerchief.

"How long have you been out here?" Marjorie asked.

"Fifteen, twenty minutes," she blubbered. "I don't know."

"You're carrying an overnight bag," Marjorie noted. "Where are you going?"

"I'm not staying here tonight," she choked

out between the tears. "I can't. Not with him. Not after the things he said. I'm taking the speedster and going to Hamilton."

"But the regatta's in town," Marjorie pointed out. "All the hotels in Hamilton are booked. Creighton and I checked today."

"Don't worry. I know lots of people in Hamilton," Griselda answered vaguely.

I'm sure you do, Marjorie thought to herself. *The people you know are half the reason you're in this mess.*

Marjorie, however, refrained from commenting. She merely lent Griselda a hand as she made her way down the remainder of the steps. "What about the rest of your things?"

"I'll send someone for them." She began to sob heavily. "Or . . . or . . . or . . . or . . . I'll come back for them in the morning. I always say I'm leaving, but I always come back . . . I always come back! I love him, but God — I hate him!"

Marjorie watched as Griselda headed off down the path to the cliff-side steps. Marjorie intended to follow, to ensure that Griselda did not fall, until she noticed a figure seated crossed-legged on the lawn. A few feet away, she could see the silhouette of a cat happily chasing low-flying insects.

"Creighton?" Marjorie called. "Creighton?"

"I'm here," he answered.

Marjorie slipped out of her shoes and ran to him. "Oh, Creighton! Thank goodness!" she exclaimed as she fell onto the ground at her husband's side. "I've been looking for you."

"I'm sorry, Marjorie," Creighton apologized and embraced her tightly.

"Don't be silly," she soothed. "You couldn't help it."

"I can help my temper, darling, and I should have. It's not like my father's behavior should come as a surprise to me. Not after all he's done."

"I don't think his behavior was so much a surprise as it was disappointing," she commented.

"Perhaps," Creighton allowed before sighing deeply. "I'm sorry we came here, Marjorie. I'm sorry we stayed tonight. We should have taken our things and headed on the next steamship out of here."

"And then you would have felt badly because I was seasick," she reasoned.

Creighton laughed weakly. "Yes, I probably would have."

"Not 'probably.' Definitely."

There was a long pause before Creighton

spoke again. "I'm still sorry I lost my temper. I could have —"

"But you didn't," Marjorie interrupted.

"I know, but I was there again, Marjorie. I was eight years old again and listening to him and my mother argue. She had been sick for what seemed like an eternity. And he . . ." Creighton swallowed hard before starting again. "My mother had discovered that my father had been having an affair. I listened from outside the door as he disclosed every disgusting detail. The things he said to her . . ."

Marjorie took him in her arms and held him tightly.

"She died the next morning," he continued after some time had passed. "We buried her three days later. Through it all, he never shed a tear. And I could never look at him the same way. Odd thing is, he never looked at me the same way either."

Creighton inhaled sharply. "If Selina hadn't stepped in tonight, I'm terrified to think of what I might have done. I'm still terrified . . ."

"It'll be alright, darling. We just need to get you out of here," Marjorie asserted. "We need to get you out of here as soon as possible."

TEN

Located on the west side of the building, Marjorie and Creighton's bedroom was hidden away from the bright rays of the morning sun. Instead, daylight crept slowly through the shuttered windows, basking the room in a warm, soft glow.

Despite the distress caused by the previous night's events, Creighton had managed to enjoy a few hours of fitful slumber. Marjorie, on the other hand, had lain awake for hours until finally succumbing to her tiredness some time just before dawn.

As the bedside clock ticked slowly toward eight, Creighton pulled back the covers and, trying not to awaken his sleeping wife, tiptoed into the bathroom. He turned on the tap, splashed some cold water on his unshaven face, and prepared himself for the day ahead. He desperately wanted to leave the island, but Griselda's departure in the speedster the night before had left him and

Marjorie, for all intents and purposes, stranded.

He had overheard Griselda tell Marjorie that she might return in the morning, but the elaborate nature of Griselda's makeup and wardrobe told Creighton that her morning ablutions were not of the speedy variety and that "morning" in this specific context did not mean "prior to noon" insomuch as it indicated "any time prior to lunch." In any event, Creighton wanted to ensure that he and Marjorie were packed and ready to leave the moment Griselda's red-lacquered toes stepped foot on Black Island.

Creighton stretched, yawned, and staggered back to his wife's bedside. Sitting on the edge of the bed, he leaned down and gave her a gentle kiss on the forehead.

Marjorie stirred slightly and rubbed her eyes.

"Good morning," Creighton said softly. "I know you didn't sleep much but —"

His voice was drowned out by a woman's frantic shrieks.

Marjorie bolted upright. "What was that?"

Creighton had leapt from the bed and was hastily donning a white undershirt to accompany his blue-striped pajama pants. "I don't know, but it came from downstairs."

Marjorie threw a bed jacket over her sleeveless peach silk nightgown and followed her husband into the upstairs hallway. Outside their bedroom door, the members of the house party — all in various stages of dress — were hurrying toward the main staircase.

Prudence, her hair in rollers and her plump frame draped in a voluminous floral caftan, caught up with Marjorie. "Thank goodness it wasn't you!" She scanned the small group. "Cassandra's here. That means it must be Griselda!"

Marjorie shook her head. "She left last night. It's Selina!"

The party hastened down the flight of cedar steps and along the hallway. Edward, fully dressed in a pale yellow polo shirt and linen trousers, led the way. Creighton, who along the way had armed himself with a heavy bronze statue, followed him closely, while Marjorie, Prudence, and a red-kimonoed Cassandra trailed a few paces behind them. Mr. Miller, his shirt-sleeves rolled above the elbows, his brown trousers unbelted, and his face covered in shaving cream, brought up the rear.

The group rushed into the dining room to find Selina seated in one of the dining room chairs, weeping uncontrollably. A mop lay

72

on the floor beside her chair, and George stood over her, a strong comforting arm wrapped around her shoulders.

"What's wrong?" Creighton posed.

George shook his head. "I came running when I heard her scream. I made her sit down, thinking it would calm her. But I can't get her to say anything."

The back door slammed, followed by the clicking of high heels on the polished cedar floor. Griselda, sporting a wide-brimmed sun hat and yet another fancy swimsuit — this time in black and white — entered the dining room at breakneck speed. "What's going on?" she asked breathlessly. "I could hear the screams all the way across the lawn."

"Griselda?" Marjorie uttered in surprise. "I thought you'd left."

"I did. Then I came back. I told you I always come back," she smiled.

Creighton, still clutching the bronze sculpture, crouched in front of Selina. "Selina, dear," he coaxed, "please tell us what's wrong. I know it's difficult, but please try."

Selina trembled and shook violently, but remained silent.

Marjorie rushed forward and took Selina's hands in hers. "She's freezing. I think she's in shock. George," she ordered, "go get a blanket or sweater or something. We must keep her warm."

George nodded and took off like a shot.

"I'll go get some brandy," Prudence announced and headed to the study.

"Someone get some whiskey too, eh?" Creighton requested.

"Why? Is whiskey better than brandy for cases of shock?" Miller asked before leaving to fetch the whiskey bottle.

"No," Creighton replied flatly. "I simply don't like the taste of brandy in the morning."

In the midst of the commotion surrounding Selina, the small black cat appeared at Marjorie's feet. He meowed loudly and with a dirty paw, pulled at the hem of Marjorie's nightgown.

"Sorry, puss, but I'm busy now," she shooed.

The cat didn't move a muscle except to pull, once again, at her nightgown. This time, he caught the material on his claws.

Marjorie sighed heavily and reached down to free the feline from the garment. As she did so, she noticed that his paw had stained her nightgown a reddish brown. "Are you hurt, puss?" she asked, recalling the kick that Cassandra had given him the night before. "Are you . . . ?"

Marjorie felt the blood rush from her head and she wondered if she might be sick. Swallowing hard, she reached behind her, grabbed Creighton by the shoulder and shook him.

"What is it?" he answered testily.

Marjorie said nothing, but pointed at the floor beneath her feet.

Creighton looked down. "The cat? Yes, what about the . . . ?" his voice trailed off as his eyes traced the cat's paw prints to a pool of blood that had collected beneath the Italian cassone.

Creighton stood up and motioned to George, who had returned from the cottage with a thick down quilt. George promptly wrapped the coverlet around his mother, helped her out of the chair and, with Mr. Miller's assistance, escorted her from the room.

Taking a deep breath, Creighton stepped toward the trunk, bent down, and with one hand, slowly lifted the lid.

"Oh, God." He stepped back quickly, letting the bronze statue slip from his fingertips and fall to the floor with a deafening clang.

Marjorie rushed to his side. There, in the open trunk, lay the tuxedo-clad body of Creighton Ashcroft II. His eyes and mouth

75

were open and his body bent and knotted to fit into the tight confines of the chest. A wide, deep wound on the back of his head and a trail of dried blood emanating from one ear proved to be the most likely sources of the blood on the floor.

Prudence gasped in shock, while Griselda let out a piercing scream.

"I-I'll go to Hamilton and get the police," Edward announced.

"No!" Creighton shouted. "No one's leaving the island. And certainly not alone. Not until we know who did this."

"Are you suggesting that . . . that one of us . . . ?" Prudence drew a hand to her chest in complete horror.

"There's only one way on and off this island, Pru," Creighton answered. "You know that."

"The killer could have hired a boat," she argued.

Creighton shook his head. "Someone would have heard them. Marjorie and I hitched a ride on one of those 'hired boats' yesterday morning."

"My hearing still hasn't fully returned," Marjorie noted.

Creighton nodded in agreement. "Nope, unless somebody paid Johnny Weissmuller to swim out here, kill Dad, and swim back,

76

I think we're looking at an 'inside job.' "

"How can you be so glib?" Edward said accusingly. "Father's dead — murdered — and we need to contact the authorities."

"Yes, we do. And, yes, we will," Creighton stated. "There's a flare gun on the speedster, isn't there?"

"Yes."

"We'll fire it off the pier — together, so that if one of us is the murderer, he's not tempted to hop in the speedster and take off. Then we wait for the authorities to arrive," Creighton explained. "Are the extra flares still behind the stables?"

"They are unless you set them off with the Ziegfeld girls," Edward quipped.

Creighton rolled his eyes. "Now who's being glib?"

ELEVEN

Emily Patterson stepped out onto the front porch of her Victorian home, a cup and saucer in one hand and the early edition of *The Hartford Courant* in the other. Her plans to enjoy a leisurely summer morning sipping tea and perusing the paper were cut short when she spotted a man lying on her porch swing.

Stuffed into an ill-fitting crumpled brown suit, the man's bulky torso occupied the whole of the swing's bench seat, leaving his limbs to dangle awkwardly over the back and arm rests. A brown fedora covered his face.

The man snored loudly and attempted to roll over, thus sending his hat, and himself, tumbling onto the gray porch floor with a thud.

"Officer Noonan!" Mrs. Patterson exclaimed as the face of her overnight guest was revealed.

Noonan sat up, blinked his eyes, and shook his head several times.

She placed her cup of tea and newspaper on an enameled outdoor table and hurried across the porch to check on him. "Are you okay?"

"I'm fine," Noonan replied as he stiffly rose to his feet.

"Are you sure?"

"Oh yeah, it takes more than a fall from a porch swing to keep ol' Noonan down." He placed a hand on his lower back and grimaced.

"What are you doing here?" Mrs. Patterson questioned. "Were you on that swing all night?"

"Not all night," he answered and moved his hand from his lower back to his neck. "But long enough."

"Oh, my! Let me get you some tea, Officer. And some of my homemade scones with fresh strawberry preserves. You must be starving!"

Tea was a beverage Noonan typically reserved for when he was getting over the grippe. However, he smiled graciously. "Thanks Mrs. P, that's awfully kind of you."

"Nonsense," Emily Patterson dismissed as she opened the screen door and stepped inside. Within moments she peeked her head around the door: "And please, call me 'Emily.' Just because we're not drinking martinis at Kensington House, doesn't mean we have to go back to calling each other by our last names."

Noonan laughed. "Well, I didn't want to say nothing. Just in case it was the vermouth talking that night. But okay . . . Emily."

She flashed a satisfied grin and went back into the house.

In the meantime, Noonan plumped the porch swing cushions, removed his suit jacket, laid it over the back of the swing, and had a seat. There, in the sun-soaked serenity of Mrs. Patterson's front porch, he could forget about the events of the previous evening and his miserable failure.

He stretched his legs out, placed his arms behind his head and closed his eyes. The breeze that whispered across his skin was warm, but dry — a welcome respite from the New England humidity, and each breath he took was fragrant with the scent of the wild roses that grew in Mrs. Patterson's side yard.

Yep, he thought, today was going to be a good day. After tea and scones with Emily, he would stop by the drugstore and pick up a few licorice twists for the kids and that face powder Mrs. Noonan had been talking about for months (she'd heard it would make her skin look like Claudette Colbert's) but still couldn't justify purchasing. Then he'd head home, play some ball with Patrick Jr., take his daughter, Nora, for a ride in her red wagon, and then — if the chicken was big enough — Mrs. Patterson could join them for dinner.

If the chicken was big enough? Noonan nearly laughed out loud, for according to Mrs. Noonan, the chicken was always big enough. Sometimes she added an extra potato. Other times, she baked an extra loaf of bread. On a few occasions, when Noonan was between paychecks or she wasn't given sufficient notice, Mrs. Noonan simply did without, supplying her guests with the simple, yet gracious, explanation that she "wasn't very hungry" after partaking of a large lunch. Noonan, however, knew that there were no such lunches; the only lunches his wife ever had the opportunity to enjoy were the crusts from their children's sandwiches.

Whatever the case, Patrick Noonan never ceased to marvel at his great fortune. An Irish Southie who dropped out of school after the sixth grade, he had a job with the Hartford County Police, two beautiful children, and he'd married a smart, pretty woman who was a good mother and never turned a hungry guest away from her doorstep.

The sound of singing birds adding to his happiness, Noonan sighed contentedly — until he spied something moving in the shrubs just outside the porch.

That "something" quickly jumped upon the porch railing with a loud "meow" and glared at Noonan with bright yellow eyes.

Noonan leapt to his feet. "You!" he shouted threateningly. "You — you — you —"

Mrs. Patterson returned with a tray of tea, milk, sugar, scones, strawberry preserves, cream, and all the appropriate serving tools.

"You — you — wonderful woman!" he inserted, moving Emily's teacup and newspaper to make room for the tray.

The cat lingered several seconds before jumping back into the bushes from whence he had come.

"What, this?" Mrs. Patterson said humbly. "Oh, it was nothing. I put the strawberries up myself after our fair. But what's strawberry preserves without a good scone and a cup of tea?"

She deposited the tray and took a seat on the porch swing. "Was that Sam I just saw?"

Noonan played dumb. "Who?"

"Marjorie's cat, Sam. There was a cat right there on the ledge. Looked just like him." She dispensed a cup of tea to Noonan and then went on to freshen her own cup. "But, of course, it couldn't be, could it? Not with you on the case."

"On the case?" he repeated, fearful that the elderly woman had seen through his antics over the past two days.

"Yes, you've been watching Marjorie's house, and Sam, while she and Creighton have been away. I'm sure she feels better knowing Sam is in such good hands." She presented the officer with a sliced scone and a linen napkin. "That reminds me," Mrs. Patterson spoke up, "you never said what you were doing out here last night."

"I was keeping tabs on, umm, a suspicious character," he explained while loading his scone with preserves and cream.

"Oh my! Here in Ridgebury?"

Noonan polished off a quarter of a scone in one bite. "Yeah, he walked right by this place, so I decided to watch him from your porch swing." He chuckled, "I guess I fell asleep."

"Yes, I guess you did" Mrs. Patterson answered distractedly. "What did this person look like?"

Noonan wiped the corners of his mouth.

"Small, wiry, gray hair, and green eyes with
—" he was about to say "with yellow bits"
but recalled Jameson's reaction the previous
afternoon. "Green eyes."

"What do you suppose he was after?"

The worry in the old woman's eyes made
Noonan feel like a heel. "Don't you worry
about him, Emily. Probably just some
transient passing through town, looking for
a job or a handout."

Emily frowned. "I suppose."

"Say, why don't you have supper with us
tonight?" he invited, in hope that it might
provide a distraction from the shadowy
figure lurking in Mrs. Patterson's imagina-
tion.

Her face broke into an immediate smile.
"That would be lovely! I can't wait to meet
your wife. Your wife does know I'm coming,
doesn't she?"

"Of course she does — she's been after
me to invite you over for a few weeks now."
As he polished off the rest of the scone, a
thought occurred to him. "Hey, do you play
cribbage? Mrs. Noonan loves it, but she's
tired of beating me."

"I adore cribbage! Although I may not be
much of a match for your wife, either."

"You can't be any worse than I am," Noonan assured her as he rose from the rocking

chair and collected his jacket and hat. "I'll pick you up at five-thirty."

"That sounds delightful! What can I bring?"

Noonan shook his head. "Nothing."

"Oh, but I must," Mrs. Patterson insisted.

"Nope. You fed me breakfast after a long night on the job. Mrs. Noonan would have a fit if you did anything else today." He donned his hat and took off down the front walk. "I'll see you at five-thirty," he called over his shoulder. "And thanks for breakfast."

Mrs. Patterson waved after her guest as he strolled off toward the green. Then, with a smile still on her face, she set about clearing the breakfast dishes. As she did so, she remembered the suspicious man Officer Noonan had described.

Poor Mrs. Wilson, she thought to herself, *she's all alone!*

Without missing a beat, she rushed through the screen door, into the front hallway and to the telephone.

"Hello?" She greeted the familiar voice at the other end of the phone. "Hello, Mrs. Wilson. It's Mrs. Patterson . . . I'm fine. How are you? . . . Oh, your lumbago is acting up again is it? . . . That's too bad . . . Listen, a policeman friend of mine told me that there's been a suspicious character hanging around the neighborhood . . . Yes, I thought you should know since you live alone . . . No, no he hasn't done anything yet . . . Just lurking . . . Oh, he's small, thin, has gray hair and green eyes . . . Yes . . . Alright . . . I'll see you at canasta next Tuesday . . ."

TWELVE

Creighton and Edward returned to the study about forty-five minutes after they had set out for the pier. Marjorie, having since traded her nightgown for a white, double-breasted sleeveless dress with a blue belt, stood at the bar cart, serving coffee from a sterling silver pot. She handed a cup to her husband as he entered. "Did anyone respond to the flare?"

Creighton accepted the cup with a loud grunt of approval. "The harbor master came by to investigate. He's going to get the police."

Marjorie passed a cup to Edward and then set off toward the kitchen, Creighton close at her heels.

"Where's Selina?" he asked.

"At the cottage, lying down." Marjorie gave the kitchen door a strong push, swinging it open widely enough for them both to enter.

"But —" Creighton began to protest.

"Don't worry, I remembered your orders. We're taking turns staying with her." She grasped a kitchen towel in each hand, opened the oven door, extracted a cookie sheet full of small, golden breads and placed them on a rack to cool.

"Scones," Creighton noted aloud.

"Mrs. Patterson's recipe. After last night's supper of hot nothing, I figured we could all use some breakfast. Otherwise, there might be nine more corpses for the police to investigate. Oh!" She threw the towels onto the counter and reached her arms around her husband. "I'm sorry, that was a horrible thing for me to say. What with your father and all."

Creighton held her tightly. "No, no. Don't be silly. I appreciate all you've done. Someone has to keep things going around here. Heaven knows, it's not going to be Griselda."

Marjorie smiled weakly. "How are you doing?"

"I'm all right. I'm not torn up about my father being dead, but, well, I certainly didn't want it to end like this." He gave her a kiss on the forehead and leaned behind her to grab a scone off the rack.

"Oh no," she turned around, snatched the

scone from his hand, and replaced it with a different one. "Take this one instead. It's an odd shape."

Creighton raised his eyebrows. "Need I remind you that one of the people you're feeding is a cold-blooded killer? I highly doubt that he or she is going to seek clemency from the court because you fed them a lopsided scone."

"I'm not worried about anyone here getting the lopsided scone," she explained. "I just don't want the police to get it."

"Why? Afraid they'll call off the investigation?" he teased.

"Nooooo," she sang. "I'm hoping that if I play things just right — butter them up, bring them coffee, feed them the perfectly shaped, light and fluffy scones — they may let me sit in on the investigation."

"No, Marjorie, not again," he whined. "I know this is an area of interest for you and I admit that you're very good at it — an expert even. But this is my father and — need I remind you? — our honeymoon. Give this one a miss, Marjorie. Please."

"I'd like to," she said in earnest. "But I can't. You see, your father spoke to me last night."

"Last night? You mean after he was dead?" Creighton said incredulously.

"Noooo," she sang again. "When he was alive!"

"Sorry. I thought maybe that Cassandra, or Rose, or Whatever-her-name-is spirit-guide-person had been rubbing off on you."

"No," Marjorie continued, "it was right after you left the dining room. I was going to look for you but your father called me back in; he said he wanted to speak with me."

"I'm not surprised. He was on a real tear last night," Creighton frowned. "So was I, come to think of it."

"He made you angry, Creighton, that's all," she excused. "I half-expected to get into an argument with him myself. I thought he'd accuse me of being a fraud or phony, like he'd done to everyone else. Only he didn't. Instead, he asked me for my professional opinion."

"Opinion? Regarding what?"

"He believed someone wanted to kill him."

"I'd say he called that one right," Creighton cracked. "Did you tell him that if he were nicer to people he wouldn't have had that problem?"

Marjorie pulled a face and folded her arms across her chest.

"No? No," Creighton deduced. "Did he give any hint as to who might want to kill him or why?"

Marjorie shook her head. "Not exactly. The day before yesterday, he had found a rather menacing note on his desk. The note had been typed and bore no signature. However, it had to have been put on his desk by someone in this house. In addition, a brief inspection of the ribbon on the typewriter in your father's office proved that the note had been typed on that very machine."

"Father never locked that office door. All of his confidential documents were stored in the safe or hidden away." Creighton sighed. "Which means that anyone could have gone in and typed that note."

"Precisely."

"Did he notify the police? They might have been able to dust the typewriter for prints."

"No, he didn't want the police involved, nor did he put much faith in their abilities. Instead, he went to a solicitor yesterday morning, and had him draw up a new will."

"You mean he was serious about that?" Creighton asked in disbelief.

"I didn't see the new will myself, but I believe he was telling the truth," Marjorie averred. "He assumed that the writer of the note was after his money; he thought he'd remove the money and with it, remove the threat. Your father believed that he had created an 'insurance policy' safeguarding against the note writer taking any further action."

"Apart from qualifying himself as the greatest prophet since Custer predicted he was going to surround all those Indians, did he tell you anything else?"

"That his new will names you as his sole heir," Marjorie stated.

"Me? You're joking. Why would he — ?"

"He had to name someone. You weren't on the island, so you couldn't possibly have left the note," she explained.

"And you? What did he expect you to do?"

"Despite all his machinations regarding the will, your father was still frightened. He must have sensed that the writer of the note was motivated by more than mere money. I think he consulted me because he wanted someone to confirm his fears, and because he needed someone to know the truth in case . . ."

"Swell. You know the truth and can pass it along to the police. Problem solved. No need for you to get involved in the investigation. No need to get your hands dirty." He punctuated the statement by wiping his hands together.

"You don't understand. Your father was murdered the same day he named you as the sole inheritor of his estate. On the precise day that you and I arrived in Bermuda. Creighton, the police are going to consider you the primary suspect."

His jaw dropped. "But the note," he argued.

"There's only your father's word that he received it when he did." Marjorie threw her hands up in the air. "What am I saying? We don't even have that anymore. It's my word only and I have something of a vested interest in seeing that you stay out of prison."

Creighton reached into the kitchen cupboards and pulled out a large serving platter. He took a well-formed scone from the cooling rack, placed it on the platter and handed it to Marjorie with a broad grin.

"Just in case," he explained. "Not that I think we'll need it. You're used to dealing with the Hartford County Police, but you have to realize that not every policeman is like Jameson or Noonan. Now, I'm going upstairs to change; I'll be back in a few minutes."

THIRTEEN

Creighton bounded down the stairs, dressed in a blue-and-white-striped twill shirt, white linen trousers, and a pair of white oxfords. He turned toward the study to find Marjorie serving coffee to two unknown gentlemen who were seated upon the overstuffed settee.

The younger and taller of the two had blonde hair, blue eyes, and might have spent his spare time modeling men's apparel for Sears Roebuck catalogs. The older man was shorter, stockier, and had a dark, swarthy complexion which, on a man of leaner proportions, might have been described as "exotic." For the stout man in the wrinkled suit, it was better defined as "greasy."

The sound of Marjorie's laughter resonated through the room. "Your mother reads my books?" she addressed the younger of the two men. "How wonderful! I'll be sure to send her some signed copies as soon

94

as we get back to the States."

"That's quite kind of you," the young man replied in a deep voice tinged with an English accent.

The older man, in the meantime, devoured his scone and marmalade with gusto.

"Oh, I don't mind," Marjorie replied. "It's the least I can do for hard-working law enforcement officers such as yourselves." She crossed one shapely ankle in front of the other and struck a demure pose.

"Goodness," the older man prompted in a Welsh cadence. "While you're at it, maybe you wouldn't mind giving my wife your scone recipe. Mrs. Jackson is a good woman, bless her heart, but she can't bake a scone to save her life."

Creighton stood motionless in the study doorway, wondering if he were truly awake.

"There he is," Marjorie stated with a smile. She waved her husband into the room. "Darling, these gentlemen are from the Criminal Investigation Department of the Bermuda Police Force." She motioned toward the older man. "Creighton, this is Sergeant Roger Jackson."

Jackson took a deep bow. "Morning, sir."

Creighton replied in kind.

"And this is Inspector . . ." she looked at the younger man, her face a question.

"Philip," he stated.

"Inspector Detective Philip Nettles," Marjorie introduced.

The younger man extended his hand. "How'd you do, Mr. Ashcroft? So sorry for your loss."

"Thank you," Creighton murmured as he shook Nettles' hand.

"I was just telling Inspector Detective Nettles and Sergeant Jackson that we've solved many a crime back in Ridgebury," Marjorie stated. "And how the police department there has come to rely upon our sleuthing skills over the past few months. But I'll let you continue the story, Creighton, while I put on more coffee."

The men stood up as she left the room. Once she was out of sight, they returned to their seats. An awkward silence ensued.

"As my wife was saying, we solved many crimes back in Connecticut."

"Mmm," Jackson responded. "Lovely woman, your wife."

"Quite lovely," Nettles agreed. "My mum reads all of her books. I'll have to tell her how lovely she is in person."

"Mmm," Jackson replied once again. "Lovely woman. Good scones, too."

"Good what?!" Creighton leapt from his seat, ready for a fight. "Oh, the, the scones.

Yes, they're light and fluffy and pleasantly unlopsided aren't they?" He sat back in the upholstered wing chair. "So, any ideas so far?"

"Ideas?" Jackson repeated obtusely.

"About the murder," Creighton clarified.

"Oh that." Jackson ate the last of his scone and brushed the crumbs from his face with short stubby fingers. "We haven't gotten in there to take a look. We told your wife we were waiting for a few more men to arrive to collect the body and, after introducing us to the other members of the household, she whisked us in here and sent everyone else to wait in the drawing room. Lovely woman, your wife."

"Yes, adorable," Creighton flippantly agreed. "Now that you've both eaten, may I suggest we move into the dining room to examine . . . things?"

The detectives briefly conferred with each other and, finding agreement, followed Creighton out of the study, down the hall, and past the young constable standing guard at the dining room entrance.

"He's in there." Creighton pointed to the carved chest that stood in the corner, its lid still propped open.

As the men approached the scene with the utmost caution, Marjorie returned from her kitchen duties.

"Who found the body?" Nettles asked. "Not your — ?"

"No, not my lovely wife," Creighton answered abruptly. "The housekeeper found him — or she found the chest, at least. When we came downstairs, the lid was closed. I don't know if she opened it, saw the body, and let it slam shut, or if the blood alone was enough to frighten her. She's been too shaken up to give us any details."

Nettles nodded his reply. "What about these tracks in the blood? They look —"

"Feline," Marjorie offered. "One of the strays on the island seems to have adopted me."

"Oh, you like cats do you?" Nettles asked in a conversational tone. "I'm more of a dog lover myself, but if you like cats, you should visit this place in town that's full of 'em. It's on . . . on . . . Roger, what's the name of the street where that green grocer is?"

Jackson glared at him and leaned over the body. "Looks like someone gave him a good cosh over the head. Probably what killed him. But we'll know more when we get him back to the morgue. Sorry it's taking so long for the other boys to arrive, sir," he explained to Creighton. "We're not accustomed to handling these sorts of things.

98

There's only seven of us in the Criminal Investigations Department and you're looking at two of 'em."

"The finest two, I'm sure," Marjorie remarked with a sweet smile.

Creighton swallowed his saliva to purge the bile inching up his throat.

"I don't know about that, Miss," Jackson said humbly. "The whole department is . . . hullo, what's this?" He bent down and, using the handkerchief from his front jacket pocket, seized a small brass statue of an angel from the hardwood floor.

"I brought that in here," Creighton explained. "Selina, our housekeeper, was very upset after finding the body. The whole household came dashing down here this morning, unsure of what we'd find." He chuckled slightly. "Habit, I suppose, from my time spent living in New York City, or our cases, but I instinctively grab something heavy or sharp before I investigate."

"Hmm. Where was it when you grabbed it?" Jackson asked.

"Oh, I don't know. It had to be somewhere between our bedroom and here, but I honestly can't remember. We were all in such a hurry. Maybe on the chest in the front hall. Why?"

"Because I believe this is the murder

weapon."

"What?" Creighton nearly shouted.

"How could that be?" Marjorie asked. "It wasn't in the room when we arrived. I distinctly recall Creighton carrying it in here."

Jackson shrugged. "Someone didn't want us to find it. They wiped it clean, or tried to. See?" He motioned to Marjorie to join him. "There's a dried substance in the etched part of the angel's wing."

Marjorie looked closely at the area indicated before her eyes caught something else. "Look. The velvet on the base is stained as well. In fact," she took the handkerchief-wrapped statue from Jackson's hand and held it so that the base was close to, but not touching, the wound on Ashcroft's head.

Jackson nodded in agreement. "They're the same size and shape. Looks like a match to me."

"Nicely done!" Nettles complimented.

"Thank you," Marjorie smiled.

Jackson took the handkerchief and statue from Marjorie's hand. "I'll wrap this up and take it back to headquarters so they can verify the match and check for fingerprints."

"Fingerprints?" Creighton cried. "If it was cleaned after the murder, the only fingerprints on there will be mine."

Jackson shrugged again. "If those are the only prints we find, then those are the only prints we find. But there's more to a murder investigation than fingerprints. We'll round up all the men in the house and find out their motives and whereabouts."

"Why just the men?" Marjorie challenged.

Jackson laughed. "You're not going to tell me that a woman lifted that man and shoved him into that trunk, are you? I know women are wearing trousers nowadays, but there are still some things they simply can't do."

"I'm not denying that a woman couldn't lift him into the chest. I'm saying that perhaps they didn't have to. Here, I'll show you. You be Mr. Ashcroft." She positioned Jackson in front of the trunk and stood behind him. "If the lid of the trunk was open, all I'd need to do is lure you to this corner of the room and whammo!" She swung at Jackson's head with an invisible statue. "Now, we all know that people fall forward, not backward."

"Of course," Jackson stated.

"Naturally," Nettles agreed.

"Precisely," Marjorie continued. "Meaning that Ashcroft falls into the trunk, well, the majority of him anyway. I bet that's what happened, too. Yes! Take a look." She

101

pointed to a set of indentations in the wall that were the exact same height as the upper corners of the trunk lid. "The weight of the body would have moved the trunk forward against the wall, while an arm, or leg probably caught on the lid, forcing it to open as far as it could go. That's how these marks were created."

Jackson scrutinized the marks and scratched his chin pensively.

Nettles stepped in, "If Ashcroft's torso was already in the trunk, it wouldn't take too much effort to roll him onto his side, fold his legs and arms beneath him, and shut the lid."

"Meaning that anyone in the house — male or female — could have done it," Marjorie completed the thought.

"It's possible," Jackson allowed. "But we don't know when those marks were made. They could be months, even years, old."

"No they couldn't," Creighton argued. "I've come here every year on holiday and that chest has never been in this room."

"That's right," Marjorie agreed. "According to my father-in-law, it had been in storage until he presented it to us as a wedding gift last night."

"Okay," Jackson acknowledged, "you may have something. I'll question every person

102

in the house, starting with you, sir."

He pointed directly at Creighton.

"Actually," Marjorie countered, "I was thinking you could start with me. I'll give you my take on events and then we can question everyone else. See how their stories fit with mine, that sort of thing."

"I think that's a bang-up idea," Nettles opined.

Marjorie smiled appreciatively at the Inspector.

"We?" Jackson repeated.

"Well, you and Nettles," Marjorie communicated. "And me."

"You, my lass, are a civilian," Jackson pointed out.

"Not if you count the number of cases I've helped to solve. Or the number of murder mysteries I've written. You've seen first hand what I can do."

"She's done as good a job as other five inspectors, Sergeant," Nettles said appealingly.

"And I can bake scones," Marjorie added. "Scones you can take home with you tonight. And a recipe you can take home to Mrs. Jackson when the case has been solved . . . by the three of us." She slid a surreptitious wink in Creighton's direction.

There was a sharp intake of breath as

Jackson mulled over his options. "Scones . . ." he could be heard murmuring before announcing. "All right, Miss McClelland, um, Mrs. Ashcroft, into the study. You're first!"

As Marjorie followed Jackson and Nettles out of the dining room, she passed Creighton a slip of paper.

"What's this?" he asked of his wife.

"The scone recipe. If we're sending some home with Jackson tonight, you'd better get baking."

FOURTEEN

"A note." Jackson mused after Marjorie had recounted the previous night's dinner and the subsequent meeting with her father-in-law.

"And all it said was 'The day of reckoning is nigh?' " Nettles confirmed.

"Yes. Typed in all capital letters," Marjorie described. "In fact, if you want to see it, it's probably in Mr. Ashcroft's jacket pocket. That's where he put it after he showed it to me."

Jackson nodded to Nettles. "Go check for the note, eh?"

The inspector obediently left the room.

"And because of this note, Mr. Ashcroft believed his life was in danger," Jackson summarized. "So instead of calling the police, he changed his will, and consulted you."

"That's right," Marjorie corroborated. "In hindsight, I wish he had called the police, but Mr. Ashcroft wasn't the type to ask for help. Indeed, I think he wanted to use the situation to his own advantage."

"So, because of this meeting, you were the last person to see Mr. Ashcroft alive," Jackson asserted.

"No, the last person to see Mr. Ashcroft alive was his killer," Marjorie corrected. "I was simply the last person to leave the dining room following that fiasco of a dinner."

"What time was that?"

"When I left the dining room? Oh, about eight-thirty."

Jackson took notes in a small black book. "Where did you go from there?"

"I went outside to look for my husband."

"You didn't know where he was?"

Marjorie silently debated whether or not she should mention Creighton's argument with his father. She had already told Jackson that her father-in-law had had words with every member of the household, but she had failed to impart the sheer magnitude of Creighton's anger.

After a few moments' hesitation, she concluded that it was better that Jackson hear the story directly from her than from the likes of Griselda or, heaven forbid, Cassandra. "Creighton and my father-in-law got into a bit of a row last night."

106

"Bad?" Jackson asked.

Marjorie nodded.

"Did it come to blows?"

"No, but it might have. Selina —"

"The housekeeper," Jackson verified.

"Yes, the housekeeper. Selina stepped in and told Creighton to go outside and cool off. Clear his head. I was about to follow when my father-in-law called me back."

"Why was your husband so angry? Because he had been cut from the will?"

The question sent Marjorie into a tailspin. If she told Jackson that Creighton was now the sole inheritor of his father's estate, it would cast suspicion in his direction. *No,* she decided. *They'll find the new will and discover the truth soon enough. Until then, it's best to let Jackson think I know nothing about it.*

"Mr. Ashcroft never revealed the identity of his solitary heir; therefore, it was premature for anyone to be upset about having been 'cut.' No, Creighton was infuriated by his father's machinations. It was apparent the old man was taking perverse pleasure in deriding his dinner guests. He enjoyed making them miserable."

"Sounds like the life of the party," Jackson commented. "So when you left the dining room to look for your husband, where did

107

you go?"

"I went outside through the back door. It's the exit closest to the dining room, so it seemed logical that Creighton may have gone that way. But he wasn't there. I even checked all the outbuildings and the grounds: no one."

"No one as in no Creighton, or — ?"

"No one as in nobody. So I came back inside and gave a quick peek in the kitchen and dining room. Again, there was no one," Marjorie stated.

"Your father-in-law was no longer in the dining room?"

"I didn't see him, no . . ."

"Go on," Jackson prodded.

"After the dining room and kitchen I decided to go upstairs. Edward, my brother-in-law, and his wife, Prudence, were in their room. I could hear them talking through the closed door as I passed on the way to our bedroom, which is next to theirs."

"What were they talking about?"

Marjorie took a deep breath; as much as she liked Pru, she knew the conversation might be valuable to the case. "They were talking about what had transpired during dinner. Prudence was telling Edward that something needed to be done about Mr. Ashcroft."

"Is that how she phrased it? That 'something needed to be done?' "

"No," Marjorie denied as the words came flooding back into her memory. "She said that she wanted him out of their lives forever. At which point, Edward promised that he would take care of him. Those were the exact words he used: 'take care of him.' Prudence responded by saying that if he didn't, she would." Marjorie frowned. "That was all I heard."

"I see," Jackson remarked. "Where did you go then?"

"Into our bedroom. Creighton wasn't there, but I got the idea to check the verandah. That's when I saw Cassandra. She was on the verandah, but closer to the other end of the house. It was a full moon so I could see her clearly. She looked very different from when she was in the study and the dining room. Something about her was harder . . . colder. And, I know this sounds silly, but she kicked the cat."

Jackson stared at her. "Beg pardon?"

"The cat I was talking about earlier, well it approached Cassandra and she kicked it. She had no reason for doing so; the cat wasn't harming anyone. And she — she seemed to smile afterwards. It was very disturbing." Marjorie punctuated the state-

109

ment with a long pause. "After I snatched up the cat, I went back downstairs. It must have been past nine o'clock by the time, because it was completely dark. I noticed a light coming in from the office; it was Mr. Miller."

"Did Mr. Miller appear angry?" Jackson quizzed.

"No, not at all," she replied. "If anything, he seemed to be relieved. And after seeing how my father-in-law treated him, I can't say I blame him. He was readying his list of references to put in the post. He and I spoke for a brief while — chit-chat really — before I went outside again, this time to the front of the house."

"Where you finally found Creighton?" Jackson assumed.

"Not before finding Griselda. She was sitting on the steps, crying her eyes out. I nearly fell over her. But I didn't, instead I helped her up and she, and her overnight bag, got into the speedster and set off to spend the night in Hamilton."

"What time did she get back?"

"That's an excellent question," Marjorie noted. "The next time I saw her was this morning, in the dining room, after Selina's screaming had garnered the attention of the entire household. Unlike the rest of us, however, she came in from outside. Looked like she had been sunning herself."

"Hmm. And, finally, where did you find Creighton?"

"Took us long enough didn't it?" Marjorie smiled. "He was on the front lawn cooling off, as Selina suggested. I sat with him and we talked for a while. Then we came inside to raid the pantry. We hadn't eaten any dinner — no one had. Creighton grabbed a bottle of wine; I found some cheese and fruit. We took them back to the front lawn, ate, drank, and watched the stars. It was going on eleven when we got back to our room."

"And you didn't hear or see anything else?"

"Not a soul and not a peep."

"And your husband?"

"You'll have to ask him, but I doubt it," she replied with an engaging smile.

"No, I — um — imagine he didn't either." Jackson colored slightly and fiddled with his collar. Nettles appeared in the doorway of the study, shaking his head. "No note, sir."

"But there must be," Marjorie exclaimed. "He put it there. I saw him!"

"Sorry, Miss," Nettles apologized. "We looked all over the dining room. Nothing. Perhaps he removed it from his pocket before he was killed."

"The typewriter ribbon," she nearly shouted. "My father-in-law was able to trace the note to the typewriter in his office because he saw the imprint in the ribbon."

"Requisition the ribbon, Nettles," Jackson ordered. "And then bring in Ashcroft's widow for questioning."

Nettles left the room and went about his duties.

"I have to hand it to you, Miss . . . Mrs. Ashcroft," Jackson complimented. "It sounds as if you can place everyone's whereabouts prior to the murder."

"Not everyone, Sergeant Jackson. Unless someone else saw them, we have no idea where Selina and George were," Marjorie stated grimly. "No idea at all."

FIFTEEN

"I was Richie's secretary for five years," stated Griselda Ashcroft as she adjusted the top of her worsted wool swimsuit. She looked at Marjorie, "He liked me to call him 'Richie,' what with his and your husband's names being the same."

Marjorie responded with a polite smile. A name was the only thing Creighton and his father had in common.

Nettles entered the room and quietly took a seat next to Marjorie.

"We finally got married four months ago," Griselda continued. She thrust the gaudy sapphire and diamond ring in Jackson's face.

The Sergeant reared back. "Yes, that's — that's very nice. Your husband must have cared greatly to have given you a ring like that."

"Yeah, he was always buying me things. He was very generous."

"Hmm. And how did you feel about him?" Jackson posed.

"Why, I loved him, of course. He was my husband," Griselda stated matter-of-factly.

"And what about his claims that you were keeping an apartment in New Jersey?" Marjorie questioned.

Griselda threw her a dirty look. "That was a lie."

"Was it now?" Jackson chuckled. "Just because we're on an island in the middle of the Atlantic doesn't mean we can't find out for ourselves. Nettles?"

"Right, sir," the Inspector replied. "I'll make those phone calls when we get back to the station."

"Okay," Griselda capitulated. "Richie was right. I am paying for an apartment, but it's not what it looks like. At least it wasn't at first. Before Richie and I were together I was seeing a fella named Benny Kerr. I fell for him — hard. But he wound up being a real crumb. Always borrowing money off of me, going around with other women. So I called it quits. That's when I met Richie and I flipped for him. It was nice to have someone give me things for a change instead of the other way around. I ran into Benny a few months back, right before Richie and I got married. He was hard on his luck, so I loaned him a few bucks. I guess part of me still had it bad for Benny because one thing led to another and, well, you know."

"You must have been quite angry when your husband outed you last night," Nettles ventured.

"I was more surprised and embarrassed at first. For him to say those things in front everyone! Later on though . . ."

"You were angry," Nettles surmised.

"That's why I went upstairs, packed my bag, and left. I couldn't stand the thought of being in the same house as him."

"Where did you go?" Jackson asked.

"Hamilton."

"In the speedster?" Nettles asked.

"Of course, in the speedster. Did you think I took a canoe?" Griselda chortled.

"Who was in Hamilton?" Jackson challenged.

"What? What are you talking about?" Griselda responded.

"You didn't meet someone in Hamilton? Perhaps Benny Kerr?" Jackson proposed.

"Benny's back in New Jersey. Would I have liked for him to come down and meet me in Hamilton? Sure," she confessed. "But this trip was so last-minute that I didn't have the chance."

"I thought this trip was your idea," Marjorie spoke up. "Selina said that you wanted to get out of the city."

"I always want to get out of the city during the summer," Griselda stated. "But we were just here in April. It was beautiful then, but at this time of year? As much as I like this place, leaving New York to come here is like going from hot to hotter."

"If it wasn't your idea to come here, whose was it?" Marjorie asked.

"Richie's. He said he needed a vacation — well, 'holiday' was how he put it. He decided to come here because of the regatta this weekend."

"Was your husband a sailing enthusiast?" Nettles inquired.

"Heavens no!" Griselda exclaimed. "But some bigwig that Richie was trying to impress was. The fella was supposed to be in town this week, so Richie made an appointment to meet with him. Winds up the guy didn't show after all."

"Do you remember this person's name?" Jackson questioned.

"I don't think Richie told it to me in the first place. Miller should know." She lowered her voice and leaned forward with a wink. "Between you and me, that sort of thing never happened when I was in charge of Richie's appointments."

"Hmm," Jackson remarked. "Getting back to last night, if you didn't meet someone in Hamilton, what did you do there?"

"I went to the bar at the Hamilton Hotel."

"Nowhere else?"

"Nowhere else," Griselda stated blankly. "I chatted with a few fellas who were in town for the regatta, had a couple of drinks, and then came back to the island."

"What time was it when you returned?" Nettles asked.

"About one o'clock."

"And was Mr. Ashcroft alive and well when you went to bed?"

"I have no idea," she shrugged. "I took my overnight bag to the only empty guest room and stayed there for the night."

"Did you hear anything unusual during the night?"

"No, but between the crying and the booze, I was pretty much out cold. Next thing I remembered was waking up with the sun. I couldn't go back to sleep because it was too bright and the room was getting warm. So I went to our bedroom to change into my sunbathing outfit. Richie wasn't there and the bed was made. But that wasn't anything unusual. He never slept very much and when he did, he always made the bed afterwards. He said no one else tucked the

117

sheets and blankets in the way he did: all the way around instead of just at the corners."

"Fascinating," Jackson commented absently.

Griselda looked around at her audience, her face a question. "Is that all? Because I can't think of anything else to tell you and I'd really like to get back to my sunbathing."

"Why do you need to sunbathe when you're covered in bottled tanning solution?" Marjorie asked curiously.

"Because until I can get tanned by the sun, I don't want to look like pasteurized milk," Griselda replied cattily. "You should try it some time." With a tug at the seat of her swimsuit, she stood up and sashayed toward the door.

SIXTEEN

"I don't know what to tell you," Herman Miller stated humbly. "I grew up in Philadelphia, graduated from Lafayette College in 1920, and tried my hand at writing the great American novel. When that didn't pan out, I put my typing skills to use as a secretary. I started working for Mr. Ashcroft about five months ago, right before his and Mrs. Ashcroft's wedding."

"What were you doing here in Bermuda?" Jackson raised.

"It was Mr. Ashcroft's idea. He had made arrangements to meet a representative from the English Steel Corporation who was going to be in town for the regatta. Mr. Ashcroft thought it would be handy to bring me along to help with any paperwork that might ensue."

"Was it handy?"

Miller crossed his legs and shook his head. "No, the man we were supposed to meet didn't show. He wound up cancelling his trip."

Jackson mirrored the leg cross. "What was this man's name?"

"Morrison. Kenneth Morrison."

Jackson jotted the name in his little notebook.

"Mr. Ashcroft and I were to meet him for lunch at the Inverurie Hotel, where he was supposed to be staying," Miller explained. "We went there and waited a good half hour for the man, but he didn't show. When I asked the front desk to page him, they told me he never checked in."

"Is that why Mr. Ashcroft was so irritated with you last night?" Marjorie questioned. "Because you had made, what was the term he used, a 'sham' of an appointment?"

"Oh, I didn't make the appointment," Miller corrected. "Mr. Ashcroft did. However, he was irritated by the fact that I hadn't confirmed the meeting. If I had, it would have saved us the better part of the afternoon. Add to the fact that I was late for dinner —"

"Why were you late?" Nettles inquired.

"I overslept. It was a very hot day, so I went to my room after lunch, to lie down."

"You slept all afternoon and were still late for dinner?"

120

"Well, I didn't fall asleep right away and then I woke up several times."

"Oh?"

"No." Miller's eyes darted to Marjorie and his face colored slightly. "The house was, um, noisier than anticipated."

Marjorie blanched as she realized that Miller's room was adjacent to hers and Creighton's. "So, Mr. Miller," she said loudly, before Jackson or Nettles could inquire as to the nature of the aforementioned "noise." "Where did you go after you left the dining room last night?"

"The office to gather up some personal items and to type my list of references. I did stop back into the dining room for a brief moment, after Mrs. Ashcroft left it."

"Why?" Jackson probed.

"To give Mr. Ashcroft my key to the New York office. And to tell him that I would be leaving first thing in the morning."

"Really? What was he doing when you saw him? What did he say?"

"He didn't say anything. He was seated at the head of the table, drinking — a glass of port, I think. He simply put his hand out, collected the key, and then put it in his jacket pocket."

"Nettles," Jackson addressed the Inspector, "when you looked in Mr. Ashcroft's pocket for the note, did you find a key?"

"No, sir. All his pockets were empty."

"But I saw him put it in there," Miller insisted.

"Shh," Jackson ordered. "Simmer down. What did you do once you left the dining room?"

"I went back to the office. Mrs. Ashcroft can vouch for me."

Marjorie nodded.

"And then what?" Jackson prompted.

"Bed. It had been a heck of a day and I wanted an early start in the morning."

"Yes, so you could leave," Jackson said contemplatively.

"That's right," Miller agreed.

"Mr. Ashcroft was a difficult man to please, wasn't he?" Jackson posed.

"Extremely, yes."

"Insufferable even, wouldn't you say?"

Miller smiled. "With all due respect, Sergeant, I know where you're heading with this. And I did not murder Mr. Ashcroft."

"But he humiliated you. Fired you."

"Being fired was a relief," Miller averred. "I had spent five months tiptoeing around the man, making sure I got my job done, trying not to get in his way, doing my best not to anger him. My nerves were worn thin. I'm glad to be free."

Jackson smirked. "I'm sure you are."

Miller's eyes grew wide. "That's not what I mean! I —"

"Thank you, Mr. Miller," Jackson interrupted. "If we need anything else from you, we'll let you know. Nettles, please escort Mr. Miller back to the drawing room. Thank you."

SEVENTEEN

"I confess. I'm guilty," Prudence Ashcroft sobbed into an embroidered handkerchief.

"What!" Jackson exclaimed.

Marjorie held a hand up to silence the Sergeant and placed the other on her sister-in-law's shoulder. "Pru, darling, what are you talking about?" she asked in alarm.

"I wished my father-in-law dead and now he is!" she shrieked.

"Pru, calm down, honey," Marjorie soothed. "You don't know what you're saying."

"Yes, I do. Cassandra taught me that our thoughts can be as powerful as any weapon and we should control them carefully. She's going to be very disappointed in me!"

Marjorie recalled the spiritual guide's face as she kicked the cat across the verandah. "I wouldn't worry, I'm sure even Cassandra's foot has slipped once or twice."

"Oh no, it hasn't. It couldn't! She's a pure

soul, unlike me." With trembling hands, Pru brought the handkerchief to her nose and began to cry hysterically.

Marjorie did her best to calm Prudence, but nothing seemed to help.

"Mrs. Ashcroft," Jackson begged, "you need to settle down, Ma'am. Is there anything we can get you?"

Prudence reached a hand into the pocket of her surplice front day dress and extracted two prescription bottles. "Water, please. I need my pill," she choked out as she fumbled with the cap.

"Nettles," Jackson ordered, "go fetch a pitcher of water and some glasses."

Before he could leave the room, Marjorie shouted, "Wait!"

As Nettles obediently came to a halt, Marjorie snatched the opened bottle from Pru's tenuous grasp. "Seconal? Where did you get this?"

"The doctor," she sobbed. "The doctor Edward and Father took me to prescrib—prescribed them."

Livid, Marjorie picked up the second prescription bottle, which was suspiciously unlabeled. Inside were twenty or so small white tablets. "And these? What are they Pru? Where did you get them?"

Prudence covered her face and began to bawl.

Marjorie grabbed her wrists firmly and looked her in the eyes. "Prudence, I'm not angry with you. Just tell me what these are."

"I don't know," she blubbered. "Gris . . ."

"You got them from Griselda?"

"To lose weight so that Edward — Edward would love me — love me again."

"They're Benzedrine," Marjorie concluded aloud. "How many of each have you taken today?"

Prudence pointed to the bottle of Benzedrine, "Three." She moved her finger to indicate the Seconal. "I — I can't remember."

"We need to get her to a doctor," Marjorie asserted.

Jackson summoned the Inspector's assistance yet again. "Nettles, are the boys from headquarters here yet?"

"Yes, sir. When I went to look for the note, they had just arrived."

"Good. Have the Constable who was standing guard use one of the boats to take Mrs. Ashcroft to the hospital."

Nettles helped Prudence from her chair and took the prescription bottles from Marjorie. As they made their exit, Edward appeared in the doorway of the study.

126

"What's going on in here?" he demanded. What are you doing with my wife?"

"She's going to the hospital," Jackson said matter-of-factly.

"Is she sick?"

"Yes. And she may get sicker."

"I'm going with her."

"No you don't!" Jackson grabbed Edward by the arm. "You're staying here to answer a few questions."

Nettles, having passed custody of Prudence on to the Constable, blocked the doorway.

Edward relented and made his way to one of the upholstered wing chairs. When he spotted Marjorie seated on the settee he stopped in his tracks. "What is she doing here?"

"She's assisting us with our investigation," answered Jackson.

"My brother's wife is assisting you, the police?"

"The new Mrs. Ashcroft has been quite helpful." Nettles replied.

"I'm sure she has," Edward said sarcastically. "Probably defending my brother while simultaneously making the rest of us look as guilty as sin."

"You don't need any help in that area," Marjorie stated sternly. "How long have you been feeding your wife Seconal?"

The color drained from Edward's face, leaving it a gray-tinged hue. "How do you — ? Is that why she — ?"

"Is going to the hospital?" Marjorie completed. "Yes. That and the Benzedrine she's been mixing with it."

Edward lowered into the wing chair. "Benzedrine? I don't know what that is . . ."

"It's for weight loss," she replied. "Which explains why both Pru's evening gown last night and her dressing gown this morning were much too big for her."

"I didn't know."

"Didn't know that she was trying to lose weight to make you happy? To make you love her again?" Marjorie shook her head. "You married Pru. You, of all people, should know that she's impressionable. Sensitive. That's why you made her take the Seconal."

"The Seconal was prescribed by a doctor my father recommended; we took her to see him about two years ago. Pru didn't like the number of hours I put in at the office. She didn't like living with my father. When she . . . was going to have a baby . . . and then lost it, she became inconsolable. She'd go to cocktail parties and start crying for no reason. We couldn't let her be seen like that — in that state. My position with the company is all I have; all I've ever had. Her outbursts were talked about for days afterward. They were bad for business and our family's reputation."

"So you asked your father for advice," Marjorie deduced.

"I shouldn't have. I know that now. My father was only looking out for his own interests." Edward's face grew hard. "Everything I've wanted all these years, everything I've believed in . . . it was all a lie. I did everything he asked — everything! I worked like a dog at his company, stayed on at the house — gave up so much — only to be cheated in the end."

Marjorie gave a start. *Was it possible Edward knew the terms of his father's new will?* "How do you know you've been cheated?" she asked. "Your father never told us who was going to inherit."

"Come now," Edward scoffed. "I'm not a fool. I know the game by now; fish of one brother, fowl of the other."

"And now there's a third brother in the mix," Jackson introduced.

"Yes, poor George. He's a good lad — too good to be mixed up with this lot."

"Tell me, Mr. Ashcroft," Jackson started, "when did this disillusionment start? Surely, the sentiments you've expressed did not sprout overnight."

"No," Edward confessed, "they've been brewing for several months now. I thought things would be different after Creighton left the company and moved to Connecticut. Between Father and me, I mean. But things were exactly the same as they had been."

"Then why did you come on this trip?"

"Because my Father was scheduled to meet with the head of the English Steel Corporation. If we, an airplane parts manufacturer, could have formed a partnership with them, it would have been the most important business deal we'd ever made."

"English Steel? You mean the appointment that fell through?" Marjorie clarified.

"Yes. I'm still baffled by that whole incident. The man went through the trouble of sending a telegram and then he doesn't show up."

"What? Who, Morrison?"

"Yes. Pru and I and . . . Cassandra . . . arrived a day ahead of my father. When we got here, there was a telegram waiting for us, confirming the time and place of the meeting." Edward shrugged. "The only explanation I can think of is that Morrison was detained by a family emergency or a last-minute illness. I suppose we'll find out more when we get back to New York."

"Mmm," Jackson noted absently. "Tell us your movements yesterday evening."

"Well, following dinner — or what should have been dinner — I went to the drawing room. After my outburst, I wanted to get away from everyone. My solitude was short lived; George joined me a few minutes later. He was stewing, and I can't say I blame him."

"Did you happen to notice the time?" Marjorie asked.

Edward shook his head. "No. But if it helps, shortly after George came in, we heard you leave the dining room and go out the back door."

"How did you know it was me?"

"We saw you through the drawing room window. You took the gravel path that leads to the stables and Selina's cottage."

Marjorie nodded. "That's right."

"So, your conversation with George," Jackson changed track. "What did you say to each other?"

"Conversation?" Edward repeated with a wry smile. "Commiseration was more like it. We both had our reasons for despising our father, and we discussed them in detail."

"Is that all you discussed?"

"If you mean, did we decide to team up

and murder the old man? No. However, we did discuss Selina. George was disappointed that his mother hadn't confided in him. So disappointed in fact that he was considering leaving the island right there and then and never returning."

"Apparently you talked him out of it," Nettles noted.

"I had to. You see, after my mother died, my father erased all traces of her existence. Creighton and I were forbidden to talk about her or ask questions." Edward drew a deep breath. "I didn't want my father to come between George and his mother, too. So I advised him to go talk to her."

"Did he?"

"I believe so. At least that's where he said he was going. When he left the drawing room, he went up the path to the cottage."

"And where did you go when you left the drawing room?" Jackson asked.

"Upstairs to the bedroom. To check on Pru."

"And then where?"

"Nowhere, except the verandah for a breath of fresh air. Then I got ready for bed and turned in for the night."

"And your wife?"

"She had been terribly upset by the evening's events, but she took a Seconal and went to bed as well."

"Really? That's strange." Jackson scratched his head in mock confusion. "Because if you were both sleeping you two couldn't have had a conversation wherein you promised to 'take care' of your father."

Edward's eyes shot tiny daggers at Marjorie. "I misspoke, Sergeant. I did have the conversation your informant described, but I didn't think it was important."

"Your father's been murdered and you didn't think it was important?"

"I didn't think it was important because I was simply trying to calm my wife. If I didn't say I would do something she might have —" Edward stopped as he realized the gravity of his words.

Jackson grinned like a Cheshire cat. "Thank you, Mr. Ashcroft. That will be all."

"No, wait," Edward pleaded. "There's something else. Something, I didn't tell you. I don't know if it's significant or not but . . ."

"Go ahead," instructed the sergeant.

"Pru woke me up in the middle of the night claiming she heard noises as if someone were breaking in."

"This house is on a private island. Who could possibly be breaking in?" Jackson asked rhetorically.

"That's precisely why I dismissed it at the

time but now . . ."

"Did she describe to you what she had heard?"

"I wasn't really listening —"

"Shocking," Marjorie remarked.

"— so I don't remember her exact words, but she said something about a loud thump that came from downstairs."

"At what time was this?" Jackson asked.

"I honestly don't remember."

"Again, shocking." Marjorie quipped.

"We'll be certain to speak with your wife about the sounds she heard. That is, if she's well enough," Jackson jibed. "Good day, Mr. Ashcroft."

EIGHTEEN

While Nettles went to the drawing room to retrieve Cassandra, Marjorie flopped onto the overstuffed settee. Jackson sat down beside her.

"What are you thinking?" he asked.

"That for every question answered, another three pop up in its place," Marjorie sighed.

"What do you mean?"

"Well, for starters, there was the timing of this trip. Why was my father-in-law here now, when he typically came to Black Island only in the spring? Answer: he had a business appointment in Hamilton. But that answer opens up a whole series of other questions. Why didn't Morrison make that meeting? And, more importantly, why did he confirm an appointment he couldn't possibly keep?"

"Maybe like Edward said, Morrison became ill or suffered some family tragedy,"

Jackson suggested.

"That explains why Morrison didn't show, but it doesn't account for the telegram." Marjorie reasoned. "It's several days' passage from England to Bermuda. Morrison would have known he wasn't traveling to Bermuda well before Edward or my father-in-law even left New York City."

"Meaning that the telegram should have been a cancelation, not a confirmation," Jackson finished the thought. "Do you think that's significant?"

"It leads me to believe that someone wanted to make sure that the Ashcrofts were in Bermuda this week."

"Yet out of the house on the day of the appointment," Jackson added.

"Mmm," Marjorie grunted in agreement. "Second, there's Prudence. We discovered the reason for her emotional behavior —"

"Oy," Jackson remarked. "I have to give that one to you, Miss. I don't know how you knew it was Benzedrine. I certainly didn't."

"But now we're left to wonder what she heard last night," Marjorie continued.

"Probably Griselda Ashcroft coming home," Jackson theorized. "If, in fact, Prudence heard anything at all. Given she can't recall how many Seconal she's taken, I have

136

my doubts."

"True, Prudence couldn't remember how many pills she had taken, could she?"

"Meaning she must have taken enough to knock out an elephant," Jackson quipped.

"Or . . ."

"Or what?" Jackson urged.

"Nothing. Just thinking aloud." Marjorie snapped from her reverie. "Then there's the note and the key. Both items were tucked into my father-in-law's jacket pocket and now both of them are missing. Why?"

"The note doesn't offer a handwriting sample," Jackson stated. "There's no signature."

"No, it's very formal. Very impersonal. It's odd."

"How so?"

"Well, it reads, '*The* day of reckoning.' If I were sending someone a message, I would have used the word 'your.' '*Your* day of reckoning.' However, I'm a writer, so perhaps it's just me."

"No, it's a valid point." Jackson allowed. "But what about the key? It's of no use here. Why would someone take it?"

"I confess, that one has me completely baffled," Marjorie stated.

"Well, perhaps we'll learn something when we question Cassandra."

"I wouldn't get my hopes up — not with that one. No, the people I'm really looking forward to questioning are Selina and George."

"You're right, we still don't know where Selina went after dinner. But we have some insight into George's movements."

"That's precisely it. We have 'some' insight," Marjorie pointed out. "But if George left the drawing room to look for his mother, where did he go? Edward says he saw George take the path to the cottage. But if George had, indeed, taken that path I would have seen him on my way back to the house. And, if he had met her in the kitchen, they would still have been there when I returned. So, where was Selina?"

An agitated Nettles suddenly appeared in the doorway. "Sergeant, she's gone!"

"Who? Selina?" Jackson asked obtusely.

"No, Cassandra." Nettles' brow furrowed. "Why would Selina . . . ?"

"Never mind, Nettles." Jackson said crabbily. "What do you mean Cassandra's gone?"

"Well, she's not in the drawing room, sir. And no one else has seen her since we took Prudence Ashcroft to the hospital. I think Cassandra used the commotion as her opportunity to escape."

"It's an island, Nettles! Even if the woman used FDR himself to divert our attention, she still can't get very far! Search the house and the island. And check with our man at the pier to make sure she didn't take off in that speed boat contraption."

"Yes, sir!"

Before Nettles could take action, Creighton appeared in the doorway of the study. "That won't be necessary. I found her," he announced solemnly.

Marjorie, Jackson, and Nettles lined up, single file, behind Creighton and followed him out the back door and down the white gravel path to the stables. There, in one of the empty stalls, lay the twisted body of the spiritualist. Splatters of deep crimson stained her stark white dress and matted the black hair of her chignon. A few feet from her body, in a small mound of hay, rested a steel horseshoe hammer, the head of which was covered in blood.

Jackson kicked the stall divider. "Two people bludgeoned to death, and one of them right under our bloody noses! How did this happen? And how, Mr. Ashcroft, were you able to locate her so quickly?"

"I had seen Cassandra outside when I went to check on Selina. She was wandering along the path behind the house; when

139

I passed her, she mumbled something about needing fresh air in order to get in touch with her spirit guide, or something to that effect. When I came back to the house, I overheard Nettles asking Miller and George if they knew where Cassandra was. I assumed she was still outdoors communicating with the great beyond, so I looked in the most obvious places . . . and found her."

"When did you leave for Selina's cottage?" Jackson asked.

"Immediately after Nettles took Pru in for questioning. Why?"

"Shortly after Nettles brought Pru to the study, she was taken to the hospital," Marjorie explained.

"Good lord," Creighton exclaimed. "Is she ill?"

"She may have accidentally overdosed on Seconal and Benzedrine."

"Seconal? That's a sleeping pill isn't it?"

"She's been on it for two years now, courtesy of your father and brother," Marjorie replied.

"Sounds just like them: if you can't beat 'em, drug 'em into submission," Creighton smirked. "And the Benzedrine?"

"Meant to treat respiratory problems, but some women have been known to take them for their slenderizing effects."

"She got them from Griselda," Creighton inferred.

Marjorie nodded.

"I hope she's going to be all right."

"I suspect she'll be fine," Jackson opined.

"Why do you say it like that?" Marjorie inquired.

"Prudence Ashcroft's departure to the hospital provided the killer with just the distraction he or she needed to strike again. The only evidence we have of the alleged overdose are a couple of pill bottles in her dress pocket."

"Are you implying Prudence faked the scene?"

"I'm saying that Mrs. Ashcroft is a very impressionable young woman. It is not outside the realm of possibility for our killer to have planted the idea in her mind."

"But why kill Cassandra?" Nettles asked.

"It's apparent she knew something about the murder. The killer didn't want her to talk."

"Given her background," Creighton added, "I wouldn't be surprised if she were using the information for blackmail."

"That would have required Cassandra to have been alone with the killer," Jackson pointed out. "Tell me, how is Selina feeling?"

"I don't know," Creighton answered. "That sedative your doctor gave her knocked her out cold. She was sound asleep the entire time I was there. Well, at least I think she was, I —"

"Sound asleep, eh? Then Selina wouldn't have noticed if you happened to sneak out and visit the stables," Jackson posed.

Marjorie' eyes grew wide. This was the moment she had been dreading since the discovery of her father-in-law's body.

"Wait one minute, you think that I — ?" Creighton couldn't bring himself to say the words.

"What I think is that you and I should go to headquarters," Jackson stated firmly. "There's a rumor that you stood to inherit your father's estate."

Creighton looked away.

"Ah, you knew about that? Well, I'm going to make a few phone calls to confirm the rumor and then afterwards, we're going to have a long conversation regarding your actions last night and this morning."

"But you haven't finished questioning everyone," Marjorie pointed out. "There's still George. And . . . and Selina when she wakes up."

"Nettles can handle those two on his own as well as keeping an eye on you, Miss,"

142

Jackson responded. With a firm grip on Creighton's arm, he escorted him out of the stable and along the white gravel path.

NINETEEN

Marjorie watched in dismay as Jackson led Creighton past the house and onto the stairs that led to the cove and the pier. Never before had she felt such an overwhelming need to solve a case.

She knew that, given the terms of the new will and his whereabouts during the murders, Jackson would feel little need to look beyond Creighton as the culprit behind both crimes. She also knew that Creighton's eminent arrest had already limited her access to vital evidence, thus reducing her chances of finding the real killer. There was no way around it; she had to find a way to stay involved in the investigation.

Marjorie needn't have worried, for the single tear that had worked its way down her cheek was soon joined by others. And she found a sympathetic ally in Inspector Philip Nettles.

"I'm sorry." He removed the handkerchief

from his jacket pocket and handed it to her. "Once Sergeant Jackson gets an idea in his head, it's difficult to dissuade him."

"Thank you," Marjorie said softly as she took the handkerchief and dabbed at her cheek. "I can't pass judgment on Sergeant Jackson. I've been guilty of a bit of stubbornness on more than one occasion."

"He's a good policeman," Nettles assured. "And a good man. He's simply accustomed to doing things a certain way. He was a Detective with Scotland Yard, you know."

"Really? Why did he come here?"

"His wife was tired of the English winters. Jackson and the Missus never had children; it's just the two of them. So, if she's unhappy, you can bet Jackson does his best to make things right."

"Smart man," Marjorie remarked between sniffles.

"So is your husband," Nettles responded. "That's why I don't think he murdered his father or Cassandra."

"You mean, you don't think he did it?" she asked hopefully.

"Of course I don't. Like I said, your husband is a smart man. If he had murdered his father, he wouldn't have drawn our attention to the murder weapon by bringing it downstairs this morning. It's nonsensical.

Nor would he have stuffed the body into the trunk his father gave to you as a wedding gift. It's too theatrical." Nettles bit his lip meditatively. "I won't even touch upon the absurdity of him doing all of this on his honeymoon. Feelings for his father aside, I find it hard to believe he'd ruin your time together."

"Too bad Jackson doesn't share your point of view."

"He will eventually. Like I said, he's a good detective," Nettles smiled. "But, enough discussion. We'd best go inside. There's work to be done."

" 'We?' " Marjorie repeated.

"Of course. Why not?"

"Well, I thought with Creighton . . ."

"That you'd no longer be considered 'trustworthy'? I'll take the risk, if only to have access to your keen intuition," he teased. "Come on."

She followed him into the house, where they were instantly met with a red-faced young constable.

"Sir," the constable tipped his hat at Nettles. "Mr. Pooley is in the study and the others are gathered in the drawing room."

"Thank you, Constable," Nettles replied.

"Oh, and, um, sir," the constable added, "I'm sorry about the second murder. I was so busy making sure that no one left the island, I had no idea that . . ."

"That's all right, Constable," Nettles assured. "None of us have much experience with murder cases. In future, keep a closer eye on things or Jackson will have both our badges." Nettles warned turned into the drawing room with Marjorie trailing close behind.

Upon their entrance, Edward leapt to his feet. "Is it true? Is it true Cassandra is dead?"

"Yes," Nettles replied. "Murdered."

"Murdered. And the whole island crawling with police," Edward scoffed.

"It won't happen again, sir," Nettles assured him.

"How do you know it won't happen again?" Miller challenged. "I don't mean to get on the wrong side of the Bermuda Police Service, but this doesn't seem the sort of thing they're accustomed to handling. How do we know we're safe?"

Griselda who, since their last meeting, had accessorized her swimsuit with oversized red-framed sunglasses and a wide-brimmed hat, stepped forward. "The men are right. You keep us prisoner on this island so that the murderer can't escape, but in the meantime we're dropping like flies."

"First my father," Edward counted, "now Cassandra, and even Prudence. How can you be certain that my wife's alleged overdose wasn't an attempt on her life? Someone could have drugged her drink last night or," he slid his eyes toward Marjorie, "her coffee this morning."

"Me?" Marjorie drew her hand to her throat. "Why me?"

"My father told me about your background," Edward stated with a glare. "What is this, the fourth murder investigation you've been involved in? Strange how death always seems to follow you, don't you think?"

Marjorie pulled a face. "Well . . . yes it is," she admitted. "But that doesn't make me a killer."

"You may not have committed the previous murders, but I'm sure you had your hand in these."

"Yeah," Griselda chimed in. "I saw Creighton leaving with Sergeant Jackson. It's only a matter of time until they catch on to you, too!"

"This coming from the woman who's spent the day of her husband's murder sunbathing and reading Hollywood magazines," Marjorie commented.

"Look where we are!" Griselda cried.

"What else am I supposed to do?"

"True," Marjorie agreed. "If he had been murdered in New York City, you'd be better able to demonstrate your grief — with Benny in a booth at the Stork Club."

"Why, yooooou!" Griselda shrieked as she sprang forward and grasped for the other woman's throat. In a flash, Inspector Nettles grabbed her arms and yanked her back.

"Stop it!" he shouted. "Stop or I'm bringing the whole lot of you to the station."

The room fell silent.

"Good," Nettles declared. "We're going to take turns and find out where each of you were when Cassandra was killed. Now," he reviewed, "we know that Cassandra was alive when Creighton went to the cottage to check on Selina."

"Right," Miller agreed. "They met each other on the path behind the house. I saw them through the window."

"Were you here the whole time?" Marjorie asked.

"No, I went into the kitchen to make myself a sandwich. I was going to eat it outside, on the patio, but then I heard the commotion in the hallway and thought I should stay put. So I ate the sandwich at the kitchen table." He pushed his glasses farther up his nose with a neatly manicured finger. "Then I came back here to the drawing room."

"Did anyone see you in the kitchen?" Nettles followed up.

"No, but George saw me come from there, so he can vouch for where I was."

"He was in the hall?"

"Yes. Looked like he had come in from outside," Miller stated.

"Hmmm . . . and you, Mrs. Ashcroft?" Nettles addressed Griselda. "Where were you?"

"You know where I was," Griselda replied flippantly.

"Refresh my memory."

"Sunbathing and reading Hollywood magazines." She shot Marjorie a dirty look.

"Where were you doing this sunbathing and reading?" Nettles quizzed.

"In the closet," she taunted. "Outside. Where else?"

"He meant where outside," Marjorie simplified.

"I'm not talking to you," Griselda replied. She then repeated the sentiment directly to Nettles, "I'm not talking to her."

"Answer the question," Nettles ordered.

Griselda sighed noisily. "Okay, I was out front. That's how I was able to see Creighton leaving with the Sergeant."

Nettles turned his attention to Edward. "And you?"

"Upstairs. I realized that, in the chaos of this morning, I had forgotten to shave, so I went upstairs to take care of it. I had just finished shaving when I heard Prudence downstairs, in the study, crying. That's when I came down to see what was happening. You can both finish the story from there."

"Thank you, everyone. Now, if you'll be so kind as to stay here in the drawing room until further notice, I would appreciate it."

"What? But the sun is outside," Griselda spoke up. "What am I supposed to do in here?"

"Read some Hollywood magazines," Nettles quipped before leaving the room.

Marjorie made a face in Griselda's direction and then followed the inspector down the hallway and into the study, where a sullen George Pooley stood, staring out an open window.

Nettles approached the boy and shook his hand. "Hullo, George. Sit down, will you?" He motioned to one of the wing-back chairs before selecting one for himself.

George obediently took a seat while Marjorie positioned herself in the middle of the settee.

"How are you, George?" Nettles asked warmly.

George shrugged.

"Would you tell us a bit about your part in last night's events?" the Inspector urged.

"You mean the man who'd been keeping us as servants all these years was my father?" George sneered.

"Yes," Nettles replied. "I'm very sorry. That news must have been tremendously difficult for you to receive."

"I — I had always believed that my father left my mother when he found out that she was having a baby. And I have always hated him for it. Without even knowing him, I hated him for leaving a woman as good as my mother. But to find out that your father has been keeping you and your mother as glorified slaves . . ." His hands gripped the arms of the wing chair as he choked back his tears.

Nettles gave him a chance to compose himself before presenting the next question: "Where did you go after dinner last night?"

"The drawing room. Mr. Edward was there. He and I spoke about our father; he was very sympathetic."

"And then?"

"I went outside to speak to my mother."

"At what time was this?"

"About eight-forty-five."

"Are you certain?" Nettles pressed.

"Yes. I remember looking at the drawing room clock before I left."

"Really?" Marjorie challenged. "Because at eight-forty-five, I was on the path that leads from the house to the outbuildings. If you had been on it, I would have seen you."

"I — I m-must have been wrong about the time, then," George stammered.

"You seemed positive about it a few moments ago," Nettles interjected.

"I . . . don't want to answer any more questions."

"What are you trying to tell us, George?" Nettles pressed.

"Nothing. I'm not telling you anything. I promised my mother that I wouldn't."

"Not talking to us makes you and your mother appear guilty," Marjorie pointed out. "Don't do it, George. Just tell us what happened."

The young man rose from his chair with a final "No!" and stormed from the room.

TWENTY

Their questioning at Black Island complete, Marjorie and Nettles boarded one of the small boats the harbormaster had provided for the Police Service. Nettles directed the pilot to steer a course for Hamilton. Pulling away from the pier and out of the cove, they watched as uniformed policemen swarmed the property in search of clues to the murderer's identity.

"You must be glad to get out of there, if only for a little while," Nettles remarked.

"It is a relief, yes," Marjorie admitted. "Especially with our last victim having been killed in the middle of the day, in the middle of a police investigation."

"I don't think I've ever dealt with a criminal quite that bold," Nettles averred.

"Or desperate," Marjorie suggested.

"Somehow, I find that the more terrifying of the two."

"So do I," Marjorie stated in earnest.

"Speaking of desperation, couldn't you have taken George into custody? Just to get him to talk."

"I probably could have arranged something. But I'm not sure an afternoon with Jackson at the station is what that lad needs right now. With all he's learned and experienced the past few days, he's just about set to burst."

"Granted, but we need him to tell us what he knows. Especially if . . ." her voice trailed off.

"If he's the murderer," Nettles completed the sentence. "Do you think he is?"

"I'd like to think he wasn't. He's a very intelligent, polite, responsible young man but, if we're talking about these murders being crimes of passion and desperation —"

"He certainly fits the bill," Nettles interjected.

"Yes, one of the strongest motives of anyone in the house. Not to mention, we can't account for his whereabouts for either murder."

"That's right. Miller said he saw him come in from outdoors around the time Cassandra was killed."

"Exactly. However, if he is the murderer, the thing that doesn't fit is the note," Marjorie explained.

"What do you mean?"

"My father-in-law received that threatening note before Creighton and I arrived on the island. But George only learned of his paternity the night of the murder."

"Meaning that the note wasn't referring to his paternity," Nettles allowed. "However, George still had enough reason to be cheesed off prior to the night of the murder. Remember, Ashcroft had denied him the money to go on to University."

"True, but I don't think so," Marjorie shook her head. "When he mentioned it to Creighton and me, he seemed more disappointed than angry. Selina on the other hand . . ."

"Was she angry?"

"She didn't appear to be, but she certainly wanted the issue to be addressed. She even brought it up to Creighton." A gleam ignited in Marjorie's eyes, "Hmm . . . she writes the note to scare Ashcroft into forking out the money. Only the plan backfires. Between the threats and the note, she's pushed too hard. Instead of paying out tuition, Ashcroft takes away the only weapon she has left in her arsenal: George's paternity."

"So Selina murders Ashcroft," Nettles deduced.

Marjorie nodded. "Ashcroft forgot a very

important principle: that a woman will go to extraordinary lengths to protect her child."

Nettles rubbed his chin meditatively. "It fits, I'll give you that much."

"It certainly does. It explains George's reluctance to talk. And it puts a very sinister spin on Selina's words to me in the dining room that night, 'I'll take care if him.' "

"That's troubling, isn't it?" Nettles remarked with a loud gulp. "And what about Cassandra? Where does she factor into the equation?"

"Perhaps Cassandra could identify Selina as the killer."

"You have proof of that?"

"No, not hard evidence, but if you could have seen Cassandra on the verandah that night . . . she was, well, angry. I suppose that was the word I was looking for earlier. Smug. She knew something, mark my words."

"Oh, I believe you. But how did Selina murder Cassandra? She's been asleep all day."

"You've never pretended to be asleep?" Marjorie challenged. "There were several times today where she was left unattended. She could easily have seen Cassandra from her cottage window, followed her to the

157

stables, and bam! Or . . ."

"Or she could have asked George to do it," Nettles assumed.

Marjorie nodded again, this time somberly. "When did the doctor say we could talk to Selina?"

"This evening. We'll do it as soon as we get back to the island."

As Nettles made this announcement, the pilot brought the boat to rest in Hamilton Harbor and tied off to one of the many cleats that lined the dock area.

After instructing the boat pilot to wait for them, Nettles and Marjorie set off on the short walk to the Hamilton Police Station. The station was a small, gray, two-story limestone building at the corner of a busy intersection. Nettles escorted Marjorie across the carriage- and bicycle-filled street and up the station steps, where the voice of Sergeant Jackson wafted through the open windows.

The pair stepped inside to find Jackson, seated at a large mahogany desk, a telephone receiver to his ear. "Yes . . . well, that's very interesting, doctor . . . and when can we speak to her? . . . what do you mean she refuses to speak to anyone? . . . yes, I know her mental state is fragile . . . yes, but . . . well, she's a suspect in a murder investigation . . . no, I understand you need to guard your patient's health . . . very well, then . . . I will call again tomorrow to see how Mrs. Ashcroft is progressing. Good day." He slammed the phone back onto its cradle.

"You two won't believe this," Jackson greeted Marjorie and Nettles. "Although there were traces of Seconal and Benzedrine in her bloodstream, Prudence Ashcroft did not suffer an overdose."

"That's good news," Marjorie declared. "Yet somewhat puzzling . . ."

"There's more," Jackson continued. "She refuses to speak with the police because doing so is too distressing. Ridiculous! Her doctor, whom I just spoke with, backs the decision. Doesn't he realize that I have two corpses on my hands? The fool should have his medical license taken away."

Nettles rolled his eyes at Jackson's indignation while Marjorie stared off into the distance, deep in thought. "We may not need to speak with Prudence," she announced.

"Not speak with Prudence?" Jackson repeated. "You're just as mad as she is!"

Marjorie ignored him. "Do you have the pill bottles we took from Prudence earlier?"

"Yes. The constable brought them back here after he dropped Prudence at the hospital. Why?"

"I'd like to see the Seconal bottle, please. I'll give it back when I'm done."

Jackson looked at her, skeptically, and then retrieved the Seconal bottle from his desk drawer. "Here," he thrust it at Marjorie.

Marjorie scrutinized the details of the handwritten label provided by Goldberger's Drug Store on First Avenue in New York City.

RX: *Seconal Sodium Tablets*
FOR: *Mrs. Prudence Ashcroft*
DATE: *August 8, 1935*
DIRECTIONS: *Take 1 tablet twice a day*
QTY: *100*
DOCTOR: *H. Morgan*

Much to Jackson's consternation, she proceeded to unscrew the cap and dump the contents onto his desk blotter.

"What are you doing?" the Sergeant shouted.

"Hold on a minute," she exhorted as she placed the pills, two by two, back into the bottle. When she had finished, she paused a moment, smiled briefly, and spilled the pills back onto the blotter. "You do it this time," she told Nettles.

"Do what?" the Inspector asked.

"Count," Marjorie replied matter-of-factly.

Nettles threw her a questioning glance, but leaned over the desk and, without a word, started counting. When he was through, he stood upright and announced, "Sixty-seven."

"That's what I got," Marjorie concurred.

"I'm happy the two of you are in agreement," Jackson said with a mocking smile. "But, in heaven's name, what am I supposed to do with that information?"

Marjorie rolled her eyes. *Certainly a former Scotland Yard detective should have been able to figure it out on his own.*

She held the bottle, label side up, for Jackson the read. "According to the label this prescription was issued thirteen days ago on August 8. It also says there were initially one hundred pills in the bottle. Now, if Prudence followed the directions, there should be seventy-four pills in the bottle. Maybe seventy-three, if she took one this morning."

Jackson's eyes narrowed and his lips began to move noiselessly.

Marjorie glanced heavenward and issued a silent prayer for patience. "Two pills a day for thirteen days is twenty-six pills," she explained. "Twenty-six from one hundred is seventy-four."

Jackson's mouth formed an 'O' in recognition. "But there's not seventy-four pills. You and Nettles counted only sixty-seven."

"That's right. So where are the other six or seven pills?"

"Prudence might have taken an extra one here and there and not have noticed it," Jackson offered.

"She might have," Marjorie allowed, "but that's a lot of forgetfulness in thirteen days time. That would mean that just about every other day, she took an extra pill."

"Well, what do you propose?" Nettles asked.

"I think Prudence counted her pills this morning, just like we did. I think that counting her pills in order to determine if she had missed a dose was probably a common practice for her. It's common practice for many people, but especially for someone as emotional as Prudence. This morning, in particular, was an especially rough one. Who can blame her if she can't remember whether or not she took her pill? So she dumps the pills out, counts them and realizes that she's missing more than she should be. She's not missing one or two, she's missing a few. Quite a few." Marjorie folded her arms across her chest. "If you recall, when I asked her how many Seconal she had taken, she couldn't answer."

Nettles smiled and pointed, "That's right. The question completely unnerved her."

"Because she had no idea where those pills had gone," she added.

"I have to hand it to you, Mrs. Ashcroft," Jackson praised. "That's an interesting observation you have there. But it's all conjecture. You have absolutely no —" He stopped and did a double take at Marjorie. "Wait, what are you doing here, anyway? I thought I told Nettles here to keep you on the island."

"Nettles did keep me there, for a time. And he'll bring me back there too," Marjorie stated defiantly. "But right now, I wish to see my husband. I assume you're keeping him here."

Jackson laughed. "At last, a correct assumption."

"I'd like to see him, please," Marjorie reiterated, this time in a much sterner tone than the first.

"Certainly," Jackson replied, his nose slightly out of joint. "This way."

He led Marjorie to a back room lined with barred cells. To the far right, she could see Creighton seated on a low cot, his elbows resting on his knees. At the sight of his wife, he leapt to his feet. "Marjorie!" he called.

"Creighton!" She ran to his cell door and reached through the bars for his hand.

"Ah, ah, ah," Jackson scolded. "No manhandling the prisoner."

"Manhandling the prisoner?" Marjorie exclaimed. "I'm not manhandling. He's my husband."

"No matter. Keep your hands outside the bars, please."

Marjorie pulled a face and then returned her attention to Creighton.

"So," Creighton whispered, "how are you faring with the Bermudian equivalent of Jameson and Noonan?"

Marjorie's eyes grew wide. "That's who they remind me of!"

"As a famous writer once said, 'Are you joking? You only just noticed?' "

"Well, I've been slightly busy trying to clear you of murder charges," she said snarkily. "But now that you mention it, they're carbon copies of each other."

"Like the negatives produced by a camera," Creighton agreed.

"Their physical appearances," she listed.

"Their mental acuity," he added.

"Even their initials!" she exclaimed.

Creighton's face went blank. "Huh?"

164

"Patrick Noonan, Philip Nettles. Roger Jackson, Robert Jameson."

"Oh, that *is* strange."

Marjorie nodded. "So, I've been working with Nettles on the investigation."

"Naturally. He's Jameson in this whole thing," Creighton remarked.

Marjorie gave Creighton a mock snarl. "There are lots of things that don't quite add up."

"It's a murder investigation. I expect there would be."

"Do you get a phone call?"

"What do you mean?" he asked.

"In the movies, when a person is arrested, they get one phone call. Do you get one?"

Creighton shrugged. "Jackson asked me if I wanted to call my solicitor, so I imagine so."

"Good. But we're not calling your solicitor," she clarified.

"I'm not? Then who am I — pardon — 'we' calling?"

"We're calling Jameson," Marjorie said flatly.

"Why, are you lining up a replacement in case I get sent to the gallows?" he smirked.

"What, and go on another honeymoon? No thanks. I'm calling Jameson to ask him to do some research for me — um, us." She flashed a brilliant smile.

"You'd better not be bringing him here. Legend has it that if a person meets their doppelganger, they die."

Marjorie pulled a face. "Of course, I'm not bringing him here. I need him to make some phone calls to some people in the States."

"Phone calls?" Creighton repeated with distaste. "Excuse me if I seem ungrateful, but couldn't you make those calls from a pay-phone and save 'our' phone call for a solicitor?"

"A solicitor will defend you when you go to court in a few months. A call to Jameson could help me to exonerate you completely." She glanced at the grimy bearded man sleeping in the cell next to Creighton's. "Not to mention immediately."

Creighton followed her gaze and sighed. "All right, call Jameson. But if he wants us to name our first born after him in return, all bets are off."

TWENTY-ONE

"More Perfection Salad, Detective?" Louise Schutt offered sweetly.

"I'll take some, dear," requested the timid voice of Walter Schutt from the opposite end of the table.

"I wasn't asking you, Walter," Louise replied sharply. "I was asking Detective Jameson."

Jameson dabbed at the corners of his mouth with his napkin. "That would be terrific, Mrs. Schutt. Thank you."

"Never any trouble," Louise assured as she placed a wedge of gelatinized salad daintily on his plate.

Walter, meanwhile, held his plate out in hopes of receiving the next serving.

"And you, Sharon?" Louise asked her daughter who, despite the presence of a fifth guest, was conspicuously seated at the same side of the table as Jameson.

"Oh, I shouldn't, Mama," she refused, "I

have to watch my girlish figure."

Jameson glanced at Sharon. He was willing to bet that, in her twenty years of life, the only thing she had watched her figure do was to expand.

"Don't be silly, Sharon," Louise goaded. "Men like a woman with a bit of meat on them. Don't they, Detective?"

"Oh, um," Jameson answered, completely disinterested in anything but the roast chicken on his plate. "Yeah, of course they do."

Sharon emitted a high-pitched titter punctuated by a loud snort of delight.

Louise, in the meantime, portioned some Perfection Salad onto Sharon's plate and then absently put the serving platter back onto the table.

"Ehem," Walter cleared his throat and pushed his plate out farther.

"Oh, I'm sorry, dear," Louise stated. She picked up the platter and, with a flick of her wrist, flung a piece of salad onto his plate with an unappetizing "plop."

Walter gave a hurt glance in his wife's direction before conceding with a shrug. "So," he started as he put the dish down in front of him, "I hear there's a suspicious character on the loose."

"Hmm? Yes, one of my men, Officer Noonan — perhaps you remember him? — saw someone lurking around the green the other day." Jameson put a piece of boiled potato into his mouth, chewed, and swallowed it. "I wouldn't worry, though. Noonan's one of my best men. He probably has it all wrapped up by now."

"Mrs. Wilson said Officer Noonan slept on Emily Patterson's porch last night. That doesn't sound 'wrapped up' to me," Walter Schutt spoke out.

"What does this person look like?" Mrs. Schutt asked.

"Six foot tall, graying hair, green eyes, and a ruthless jaw," Schutt described.

"Six foot tall? Ruthless jaw?" Jameson repeated incredulously. "Where did you hear that?"

Louise Schutt gasped. "Sounds dangerous. Maybe we should put an extra lock on the shop door."

"I'm sure your shop is fine," Jameson reassured.

The Schutt family, however, would have nothing of it.

"I'll take care of the shop door first thing in the morning," Walter stated.

"I'll make sure all the doors are locked after Detective Jameson leaves tonight, Mama," Sharon proposed.

"Good idea, sweetheart," Louise praised her daughter. "And until this fellow is caught, I don't think it's safe for you to go out alone. What do you think, Walter?"

"Definitely not," Schutt agreed as he snuck more chicken and potatoes onto his plate.

"Your father's right, Sharon." Louise warned, "You never know what's on young men's mind these days!"

"Young? The suspect has gray hair," Jameson pointed out.

"Oh, I'm sorry, Detective Jameson," Louise apologized, oblivious to anything but her own family's fear. "I wasn't including you in my statement. I was talking about other young men who weren't brought up as well as you were."

"I didn't think you were including me," Jameson stated.

"What's that?" Louise feigned deafness. "You think you should escort Sharon on errands until this fiend is captured?"

"No," Jameson shook his head vehemently. "I didn't say that."

"I think that's a splendid idea!" Louise proclaimed. "What do you think, Walter? Should we let this young man take care of our Sharon?"

Walter shrugged and stole a second piece

170

of bread from the basket.

"I agree," Louise affirmed. "And what do you think, Sharon? Would you feel safe walking about with Detective Jameson?"

Sharon looked up from her plate, a piece of potato adhered to her pig-like nose. "Oh, I'd feel safe, Mama. I'd feel *very* safe," she assured and then smiled broadly at Jameson.

As the Detective stared in horror at the piece of shredded cabbage wedged between Sharon's two front teeth, Noonan's words of warning came flooding back into his memory. His heart skipped a beat as he realized that he was, indeed, the "Express Train to Marriagetown."

Just then the telephone rang.

Louise Schutt lifted her Hooverette-clad posterior from her chair and moved deliberately to the phone, which rested upon a small living room end table. With an overly sweet telephone voice, she lifted the receiver and said, questioningly, "Hello? Yes, he's here . . . oh, my, how exciting! . . . yes, just a minute."

With a girlish spring in her step, Louise hurried back to the dining room. "Detective Jameson," she addressed, "it's for you. Long distance from Bermuda. The operator said it's urgent. It must be a case. How exciting!"

Jameson took the napkin from his lap and sprinted to the living room, happy for the opportunity to end all talk of six-foot-tall marauders, door locks, modern men's morals, and, most of all, marriage.

He lifted the heavy black receiver to his ear. "Hello? . . . Yes, this is Detective Robert Jameson. Yes, I'll accept the call."

The voice that came on at the other end of the line was soft and familiar. "Hello? Robert?"

"Marjorie?" he said in disbelief. "I thought you were on your honeymoon."

"I am. I was. Look, I need your help. Creighton's in jail under suspicion of murder."

"Someone died on your honeymoon? Do people drop dead everywhere you go?" he asked, in jest. Still, part of him did wonder about Marjorie's ability to act as a murder magnet.

"I already heard that joke once today," she quipped. "It was stale then, too."

"Sorry," he apologized with a chuckle. "So Creighton's in jail. How is he? And how are you? Are you okay?"

"I'm fine. Just looking forward to the day when he and I can get back home."

"Mmm. How's the investigation going?"

"Why it's —" She paused. "How do you

know I'm involved in the investigation?"

"Intuition," Jameson grinned.

The sarcasm of his comment completely eluded her. "Really? Good for you! I always said you didn't listen enough to your gut instincts."

"Uh huh. So, what can I do from one thousand miles away, to help you?"

"I need you to do some research for me," Marjorie stated. "Do you have a pencil and paper handy?"

Jameson opened the end table drawer to find a small notepad and a red grease pencil. He sat on the sofa and, with legs crossed, balanced the pad on one knee. "Yep. I'm ready."

Marjorie listed the items requiring investigation, and then asked Jameson to read them back to her.

"That's right," she confirmed when he had finished.

"When do you need this information?" he asked.

"As soon as possible," she stated. "And as soon as you learn something — anything — call here at the station. I'll take care of the charges when I get home."

"You have the number for me?" As Marjorie recited the number, Jameson marked it, in grease pencil, on the small yellow pad.

"Okay. I think that does it. I'll get on this right away." Jameson glanced into the dining room, where the Schutts, like vultures, were eagerly awaited his return. "In fact," he said in a voice loud enough for the Schutts to hear, "I'll head down to the station and get on that right now."

"Now?" said the voice on the other end of the phone. "Who are you going to contact now? It's nearly six o'clock there, isn't it? We're only an hour ahead of you. I'm quite certain we are."

"Yes, you're right," Jameson agreed loudly. "But important police work like this can't wait."

"Oh, well, thank you, Robert," she said appreciatively. "I can't tell you how much it means to know you're willing to help us out like this. Next time you're in a pickle, be certain to call the Ashcrofts, because we'll owe you one."

Jameson turned around and watched as Sharon picked up her plate and began slurping the Perfection Salad. "No, that's not necessary," he assured Marjorie as he anticipated his escape. "I think we're square."

TWENTY-TWO

His primary suspect safely behind bars, Sergeant Jackson returned with Marjorie and Inspector Nettles to Black Island. Weary from the day's events, they passed the boat ride in silence. The silence was broken by the constable, who met them at the Black Island dock.

"Sergeant. Inspector," the tall, thin constable saluted. "The boys from the morgue are gone. Took the bodies with them. And the lads doing the grounds search have left for the day."

"They find anything?" Jackson inquired.

"A necklace, sir, in the stables. They believe it belonged to the dead woman. Constable Worth can show it to you. He's up at the maid's cottage."

"Is she awake?"

"Yes, sir. Worth's been keeping guard at the cottage until you or Inspector Nettles could question her."

"Good work, Smith," the Sergeant addressed the constable before making his way up the cliff-side staircase.

With a tip of his hat, Inspector Nettles followed the Sergeant up the stairs and across the grounds to the front door of the cottage. Marjorie, uncertain as to whether or not she was welcome during this round of questioning, followed closely behind the men.

"Sergeant Jackson," Worth welcomed. "Inspector Nettles."

"Constable Worth," Jackson greeted in return. "Constable Smith said you have something for me."

"I do," Worth confirmed as he pulled a cloth-wrapped packet from the pocket of his uniform and passed it to Jackson.

Marjorie and Nettles each peered over a shoulder as the Sergeant unfolded the handkerchief to reveal a green teardrop necklace. "This was found in the stable?"

"Yes, in the stall behind the body," Worth clarified. "We believe it belonged to the dead woman and was knocked loose by either the blow to her head or the fall afterwards."

Jackson nodded and carefully turned the pendant over. In the golden rays of the low-hanging sun, the trio could distinguish a series of symbols engraved upon its back. "What's this? Hieroglyphics?"

"No," Nettles dismissed. "It's something else."

"It's Cyrillic," Marjorie identified. Seeing the vacant expression on Jackson's face, she then paraphrased, "Russian. Judging from the light color of the jade, I'd guess that it's also Russian, most likely from the Lake Baikal region."

Simultaneously, the three men turned their attention from the necklace to Marjorie.

"The heroine in my novel, *Slaughter in Samara,* wore a ring made of the stuff. It was a great story, but since Samara isn't Samara any longer, my publisher pulled it from the shelves. Shame, really. I consider it one of my best."

"Miss McClell— er, Mrs. Ashcroft!" There was a sharp edge to Jackson's voice. "What are you doing here?"

"You mean what am I doing, aside from sharing my depth and breadth of seemingly useless information which has, so far, saved you and your men countless hours that might have been spent analyzing crime scene evidence? Nothing. Absolutely nothing."

Jackson quietly passed the necklace back

to Worth and, with an exaggerated smile and a wide sweep of his arms, motioned toward the door. "After you."

Marjorie curtsied slightly and proceeded through the cottage door.

As Marjorie sashayed past him, Jackson lifted his leg to kick her in the rear, but, thinking better of it, stepped over the threshold instead.

"Hello?" Marjorie called into the dimly lit dwelling.

"Mrs. Marjorie?" a weak voice answered.

She followed the sound to a small back bedroom. There, they found Selina, lying in a single bed, her head propped against two cotton-encased pillows.

"Hi, Selina," Marjorie greeted. "How are you feeling?"

Selina reached for the younger woman's hand. "I'm all right, child. I'm just sorry to have put everyone to so much trouble. I remember screaming and Mr. Creighton trying to calm me. He gave me brandy. Lord, now I know why I stick to rum. It's suppertime and I've only just woken up." She shook her head. "And all you poor people fussing over me."

"We liked fussing over you for a change. And you weren't any trouble. You were shocked and scared," Marjorie said softly.

178

"Anyone would have been, given what you had seen."

"I went to the dining room that morning to clean up the dishes from the night before. I didn't pay much attention to anything else around me. When I had finished with the dishes, I swept up the broken glass and came back with a mop to clean up the wine. That's when I saw the blood," Selina recounted. "Lots of blood. I should have left the lid closed . . . I should have . . ." She covered her eyes as if doing so would block the memory of her gruesome discovery.

"Don't think of it," Marjorie instructed as she clutched Selina's hand with both of hers. "Put it out of your mind now."

Selina closed her eyes and grasped Marjorie's hands tightly. "I will, child. You're a good soul. No wonder Mr. Creighton loves you." She opened her eyes and scanned the faces of the two men in the room. "Where is he? Where is Mr. Creighton?"

"Sergeant Jackson here has him locked up under suspicion of murder," Marjorie punctuated the statement with a dirty look in the sergeant's direction.

"Why? Because he was so angry? That boy and his father . . ." Selina shook her head ruefully. "Now that Mr. Ashcroft is gone, I need to talk to you about that, child. All the pain in Mr. Creighton's heart, it's all over nothing."

"Well, we can talk later," Marjorie assured. "But right now Sergeant Jackson and Inspector Nettles need to speak with you."

"All right Mrs. Marjorie, I'll talk to them, so long as I can talk to you in private later. Because you need to tell Mr. Creighton that not everything he thinks about his father is true."

"It isn't, eh?" Jackson goaded. "I suppose that's why you were so in love with the man."

"I was in love with Richard . . . Mr. Ashcroft, yes," Selina admitted. "But that was years ago. Before he pushed love aside in the name of making more money."

"Pushed love aside? Mr. Ashcroft just remarried, didn't he?"

"Oh," Selina waved the notion aside in annoyance. "He didn't marry her for love. He married her for the same reason a man buys a pair of diamond cuff links. To prove that he can."

"Sounds to me like you were jealous of the new Mrs. Ashcroft," Jackson surmised.

"When I first heard of his marriage to Mrs. Griselda, I must admit my heart did sink. It's nice, after a love affair, to believe that your beloved could never find another

180

soul to replace you. I lived under that belief for eighteen years," Selina frowned. "But when Mr. Ashcroft arrived here in April, and he announced his upcoming marriage, I was not sad. I was not jealous. He was no longer the same person I fell in love with years ago; he had changed. And so, I suppose, had I."

"Oh?" Jackson prompted Selina to continue.

"I had raised a child on my own. Of course, Mr. Ashcroft paid me my wages and gave me a stipend for George's clothes and shoes, but I handled the day-to-day living: the illnesses, the bullies, the schoolyard fights, the homework, the chores. And there were the small celebrations too: the good report cards, the first school dance, and now, his graduation." Selina smiled proudly. "Nothing takes away your romantic notions faster than raising a child alone, but nothing else makes you realize that, apart from giving you a beautiful boy, perhaps you didn't need that man around in the first place."

"You may not have needed that man around," Jackson prefaced, "but you needed his money, didn't you? You needed his money to send that 'beautiful boy' to university."

"I didn't *need* the money," Selina said defiantly. "I would have found a way to get it . . . eventually. But I didn't want George to wait. All his friends were making plans, moving forward with their lives. Why shouldn't he? Those children are no better than my son."

"So you asked Mr. Ashcroft for the money," Nettles put forth.

"Yes. He was always proud of his boys' education. He had sent both Mr. Creighton and Mr. Edward to some of the finest schools in England and the United States. Expensive schools. So, I didn't think that paying for George to go to university — a less-expensive, colored university — would have bothered him so much."

"But it did," Marjorie stated.

"Yes, it did. He was outraged. He felt that he had already done enough for me and a son he . . . he . . . never wanted. He said that sending a bastard to university didn't make him any less of a bastard," Selina broke down.

Jackson offered her a handkerchief from inside his jacket.

Selina took the handkerchief and blew her nose loudly. After a few seconds she continued her story. "I went mad, I think, when he said that. I became possessed. I started

182

hitting him, pounding him on the chest. I swore I would tell everyone that he was George's father."

"How did he react?" Marjorie asked.

"He smiled. Not a nice smile, but the smile someone makes when they are up to something. Then he took me by the wrists, pushed me away, and left the room."

"And when did this occur?" Nettles questioned as he jotted notes into his notebook.

"Day before yesterday. George had picked them up in Hamilton that morning and, during the boat ride over, Mr. Ashcroft offered him a permanent job here on the island. While Mrs. Ashcroft unpacked their things and got settled in, Mr. Ashcroft came to see me here at the cottage. He wanted to tell me about the generous offer he had made," Selina gave a wry laugh.

"Did you speak of the incident again?" Jackson inquired.

"No, not until last night, at dinner, when Mr. Ashcroft made his announcement. Despite my threats, he knew I wouldn't have told anyone. I've spent the past eighteen years keeping that secret, telling everyone that I married a boat captain and that George was a product of our wedding night. I've spent the past eighteen years lying to my boy, because I didn't want to disgrace

183

him. Mr. Ashcroft knew that and he used it to punish me."

"How did you feel?"

"I was furious," Selina answered frostily. "To tell it to the family that way was bad enough, but for George to find out like that — in front of everyone — Richard may as well have stabbed me in the heart."

"And so you wanted to stab him in his heart," Jackson proposed. "Or perhaps just grab the closest heavy object and hit him over the head."

"I did not!" Selina sat upright. "I swear to God I did not kill that man."

"No? But you wanted to," Jackson provoked.

"Yes, I wanted to," Selina admitted. "Wouldn't you? George is all I've ever had. I put my whole life into that boy and with a few words he had taken it all away."

"So you killed him," Jackson hypothesized. "You were filled with rage — not yourself. You stuffed him into the trunk before someone saw him there and then went to bed for the night. When you awoke you wondered if it had all been a dream; a terrible dream. But then you walked into the dining room and saw the blood. You screamed with the realization that it was all true. You *had* murdered Mr. Ashcroft. You *had* stuffed his body into the —"

"Sergeant Jackson," Marjorie interrupted as she jumped from the edge of the bed and onto her feet. "I will not listen to you berate this woman any longer."

"It's alright, child." Selina patted Marjorie's hand and urged her to sit down. "A braver woman might have taken the course of action you described, Sergeant Jackson. But I am not, and have never been, brave."

"Really?" Jackson replied skeptically. "Then where did you go after dinner?"

With that, George's voice came from the front door of the cottage, followed by the sound of Constable Worth trying to restrain the young man.

"Mum!" George called. "Mother, you don't need to say anything. I didn't tell them."

Jackson gave a questioning look to Nettles, who nodded his reply.

"Let him in, Worth," Jackson called.

An out of breath George appeared in the bedroom door a few moments later. "They questioned me, Mother. But I didn't say anything."

Marjorie rose from her spot on the bed and gave it to George, who accepted the seat without missing a bet. "I couldn't tell them. I wouldn't — not until I spoke to you first."

Selina's eyes welled up with tears. She leaned forward and threw her arms around her son. "Then I haven't lost you," she cried.

"You could never lose me," the young man promised. "I know why you kept my father's identity a secret all this time. I know you were trying to protect me. That's why I tried to protect you."

"This is all very touching," Jackson said sarcastically, though with a sniffle that conveyed that he had, perhaps, been moved by the emotional scene. "But we're conducting a murder investigation and neither of you have been very forthcoming as to your whereabouts the night Mr. Ashcroft was murdered."

Selina released George from her embrace and leaned back against the pillows. "As I was saying earlier, Sergeant Jackson, I am not a bold woman. A bold woman would have clawed Mr. Ashcroft to pieces that first day, when I asked him for the money. A bold woman would have, as you say, stabbed him in the heart that night at dinner. But I am not a bold woman or a brave one. I am a coward. A bold woman would have put an end to Richard's tyranny by ending his life;

I, took the coward's path and tried to end my own."

TWENTY-THREE

Selina's startling announcement blanketed the room in a somber silence.

"Suicide?" Marjorie whispered, for the volume of her normal speaking voice would have seemed, somehow, too intrusive.

"Off behind the house, to the left and off the path, there's a trail through the forest. So narrow and overgrown it is, that if you didn't know it was there, you'd never notice it." Selina's face softened as she recalled, "George was the one who created the trail. When he was a boy, he knew every last bit of this island: each tree, each rock, each little blade of grass. One day he came running to me saying he had found the most beautiful spot in the entire world. There was always work to do in those days —"

"But you always came when I asked," George rejoined. "No matter how foolish."

"I always tried," Selina qualified. "That day I was especially glad I had. George had discovered the loveliest spot, if not in the whole world, then the whole island. It was a grassy ledge, high on a cliff, looking out at nothing but the ocean. It became 'our spot.' In summers, we'd take lunch or supper there. In winter, we'd go out after a heavy rain and watch the storm clouds blow out to sea. George even said he would take a bride there someday —"

"Still planning on it," George interjected.

"— just the two of them, a minister —"

"And you, of course," George added.

"But, most of all, it became the place we went to when things weren't right — when we were sad or worried or angry. Last night, when Mr. Ashcroft told you the truth," Selina looked at her son, and began to cry, "I thought you were gone. I thought you would never forgive me, that you would hate me forever."

George patted her hand soothingly. "I was angry, but I could never hate you. It took Mr. Edward to point that out to me, but when he did, I knew I had to find you and tell you that everything was going to be fine." He turned to Sergeant Jackson and Inspector Nettles, "When I left the drawing room, I started heading in this direction and then I thought about our spot. And it's a good thing I did, because my mother was . . . was . . . about to jump."

"That wasn't my reason for going there," Selina quickly clarified. "I went there to look for George. I wanted to explain why I had lied and to ask for his forgiveness. I ran through the forest as fast as I could, but when I arrived, and he wasn't there, my heart sank. See, no matter what happened, no matter how bad things got, I always knew where to find him. For him to go elsewhere . . . well, I thought the worst. I wondered if he'd ever be able to forgive me. I wondered what I would do if he were never to speak with me again. I imagined my future without him in it: never seeing him attend university, never seeing him get married, have children. A mother gets used to the idea of her son going off into the world and making a life of his own; but to never see or speak to him again . . . and all because of something I had done . . ." She shook her head. "I couldn't bear it. So I . . ."

"That's alright, Miss Pooley," Nettles interrupted. "You needn't go any further."

"Don't speak so quickly, Inspector," Jackson corrected. "Why didn't you tell us all this in the first place, George?"

"Why didn't I tell you that my mother thought of ending her life?" George repeated in disbelief. "Isn't it bad enough that my name will be in tomorrow's paper, listed as that man's son? Do you know what all of Hamilton will be saying tomorrow? About my mother? About me? Would you want to hear those things said about someone you loved?"

Jackson looked beyond George, into the near distance, before answering in earnest. "No, son. I would not."

"Then please, let us be," George pleaded.

Jackson bit his lower lip. "I will, after one more question."

"Go ahead," the young man consented.

"Miller saw you come in from outdoors just after the time Cassandra was murdered. Where had you been?"

"I went outside to stretch and walk around — I had been in that stuffy drawing room all morning. When I went outside, I heard a scream; I immediately thought of mother, so I came here to check on her. Mr. Creighton was on the sofa in the living room and mother was here in bed. They were both sound asleep."

"Yep, that sounds like Creighton's idea of standing watch," Marjorie deadpanned.

"When I saw they were asleep and all was well, I turned back to the house. I assumed the scream was Mrs. Prudence being led to the boat. But," George's jaw dropped. "But

191

it wasn't Mrs. Prudence, was it? It was Cassandra."

"Given the timing, I'd have to say so," Nettles acknowledged.

"If I'd known, I could have gone to the stables and — and —"

"And what, George?" Selina demanded. "Gotten yourself killed, too? No, I'm glad you didn't go."

"Your mother's right," Jackson affirmed. "This isn't the sort of person you want to tangle with, if you can help it."

"But if I had caught the person, Mr. Creighton wouldn't be in jail right now," George frowned.

"You have helped Creighton," Marjorie pointed out. "By telling us everything you have, you've corroborated his alibi for the time of Cassandra's murder. Hasn't he, Sergeant Jackson?"

"He's given your husband a few minutes of an alibi," Jackson allowed. "We'll see about the rest tomorrow."

"Tomorrow?" Marjorie said in disappointment. "Can't you arrange something for tonight?"

"I'm sorry Mrs. Ashcroft," Jackson explained, "but that new will gives your husband the strongest motive of anyone here. I shouldn't need to tell you that.

However, your husband's bail hearing is tomorrow morning, so if you desperately need him back in your eager arms, then you should make sure you're present."

"Bail," Marjorie said to herself with a frown. "I don't know if I'm able to. We eloped and got married on the ship. We haven't taken care of any of the formalities, like marriage certificates and bank accounts."

"Well, then you should have used that one phone call to contact a solicitor, instead of calling your policeman friend in the States, hadn't you?"

"That phone call is going to solve your case," Marjorie vowed.

"We'll see," Jackson commented and donned his hat. "Miss Pooley, thank you for your help. George, you take care of yourself and your mother." He tipped his hat at Marjorie. "Mrs. Ashcroft, give that intuition of yours a rest this evening . . . please."

"We'll see," she volleyed as Jackson disappeared out the bedroom door.

Nettles followed close behind Jackson. "Goodnight, Miss Pooley. George." He pulled Marjorie into the living room. "We're taking Worth and the other boys back with us, but Smith will be standing guard all night." He handed her a small metal object strung onto a long cord. "Take this and wear it. If you see anything suspicious, use it and Smith will come running. Understand?"

Marjorie looked at the item in her hand. "A whistle?"

"A police whistle. It's mine, so don't lose it. But I thought it might help you to rest a bit easier tonight."

Marjorie smiled. "It will. Thank you, Inspector."

Nettles winked his farewell and followed Jackson and Worth out of the cottage and up the path that led to the house and, beyond it, to the cove. Watching from the doorway as the policemen disappeared from view, Marjorie was struck with a profound sense of sadness. So long as she was busy looking for clues and questioning suspects, it was easy to push Creighton's absence from her mind. But here, in this isolated, foreign land, with nightfall slowly encroaching, Marjorie had never felt more alone.

"Mrs. Marjorie," came Selina's gentle voice from her kitchen. She had donned a colorful pink floral housecoat and was moving carefully to the old wood stove.

Marjorie hastened to the kitchen. "What are you doing up?"

"Oh, I've been in that bed all day. I need to do something useful. Besides, it's high time we have supper."

George came in, carrying an armful of wood. Marjorie stepped out of his way as he loaded it into the stove.

"You're not cooking for the entire house, are you?"

"Oh no. When Mr. Edward heard I was awake, he came by to tell me not to worry about dinner. I told him I wasn't worried at all." Selina laughed. "But I am worried about you, Miss Marjorie. You haven't eaten all day, have you?"

Marjorie thought back to what she had consumed throughout the day. "Umm, I had half a scone this morning. And some coffee."

"Half a scone? That's not a proper meal. Where are your vegetables and your meat?" Selina lit the largest of the burners with a long match and then passed the match to George, who used it to light the cottage's gas lanterns in anticipation of the impending darkness.

"Well, I . . ." Marjorie wracked her brain for an excuse.

"You're not going to be any use to your husband if you're sick from hunger." She summoned George, who pulled a cast-iron Dutch oven from the icebox and placed it on the lit burner. Selina opened the lid and gave the contents a stir. "Fish chowder," she announced.

As if on cue, the small black cat appeared in the open front door of the cottage.

"Hello, puss," Selina greeted. She removed a hunk of dense white fish from the pot, placed it in a small bowl, and presented it to the cat, who immediately began to gobble it down.

"I see you know each other," Marjorie commented.

"Oh yes, it is bad luck to turn a black cat out of your home. Good thing this one enjoys my cooking. Hopefully you'll enjoy it, too."

"Well, I don't want to put you to any trouble."

"No trouble, child. I just have to bring it to a boil and add a few more things and we'll be ready to eat. I did most of the simmering this morning before everything happened. Good thing George thought of putting it in the icebox to keep."

"You know I hate to see chowder go to waste," George explained. "Mum makes the best chowder of anyone I know," he said to Marjorie aside.

"I thought I made the best chowder on the island," Selina asserted.

"Did I say that?" George teased.

"You most certainly did," his mother answered.

"Well, I'll have to taste it again tonight and tell you if I was lying."

Selina laughed out loud and threw a dishtowel at her son. "You rotten boy! Go get the rum and set the table for three."

Marjorie smiled broadly. It was the first display of genuine family warmth and happiness she had witnessed since arriving on the island and she was loath to leave it. However, she didn't want her presence to be a hardship on the Pooleys. "Oh, no. Only set a place for me if you think you have enough," she warned, somewhat half-heartedly.

Selina saw right through her. " 'Oh, no' Mrs. Marjorie protests," she chuckled, "but each time she breathes in, her eyes get bigger."

Marjorie laughed again. "It *does* smell wonderful. I just want to make sure you and George have enough to eat, too."

George placed a shot glass and a bottle of dark Bermudian rum on the table. "We'll have plenty. Mum makes enough to feed my entire cricket team."

"That's because you eat as much as the entire cricket team," Selina quipped.

"Can I help you with anything?" Marjorie offered.

George shook his head and took three bowls from the cupboard.

"No, child," Selina answered. "You can have a seat at the table and in a moment, when this is ready to simmer, we can have our talk."

"That's right," Marjorie recalled. "You wanted to talk to me about Creighton,"

"Yes, but first, would you like something to drink? Some tea? Or some ginger beer?"

"I've never heard of ginger beer. Nor have I ever tasted rum," Marjorie replied as she nodded to the bottle on the table.

"The rum is for the soup," George piped up as he drew three spoons from a kitchen drawer. "And Mum's tea."

"Yes, I enjoy a cup of tea with rum every evening before bed. Now Mrs. Marjorie knows my secret," she teased. "Right now, though I'd like a ginger beer. Would you like to try one? They're nice and cold."

"Sure," Marjorie accepted. "Why not? When in Bermuda . . ."

"That's right. You are about to have a true Bermudian meal. Something most visitors do not have the opportunity to experience," Selina stated as she pulled three bottles of ginger beer from the icebox and opened them.

"All the hotels serve either English or American food," George said. "Local specialties aren't an option. Even Mr. Ashcroft — my father," he added reluctantly, "never wanted anything other than roast beef and Yorkshire pudding."

"Get Mrs. Marjorie a glass, please, George," Selina instructed as she passed him his bottle of ginger beer.

"Don't bother with a glass," Marjorie told her hosts. "I'll drink it from the bottle."

Selina handed Marjorie the bottle of ginger beer and sat beside her at the table. George, meanwhile, took a sip of ginger beer and gave the pot a stir.

"You know, this reminds me of old times," Selina said with a smile. "I was a young girl, a little older than George and had just started working here. Mrs. Ashcroft — not Mrs. Griselda, but Mrs. Madeleine, the boys' mother — came out here with two bottles of ginger beer she had picked up in Hamilton. Richard was in the house working and she was lonesome."

George, his curiosity piqued, sat down at the round table, across from his mother and to the left of Marjorie.

"It became a habit with us," Selina continued. "Every time the Ashcrofts would visit, she'd come down here after dinner, or later on, after she had put the boys to bed, and we'd drink a few ginger beers — she drank it from the bottle too — and we'd laugh and laugh.

"Later, when she was ill, I'd bring the ginger beers to her bedroom and roll her chair out onto the verandah. But we never abandoned the tradition, even though she knew she was dying," Selina went on. "You know, you remind me of her, Mrs. Marjorie. Not in your appearance, but your manner. She was fearless."

"Thank you," Marjorie said gratefully. "That means a lot coming from you. Although I'm not sure I'd call myself fearless."

"Yes, you are," Selina insisted. "You working with the police in order to prove Mr. Creighton's innocence. And helping George and me along the way . . . well, Mrs. Madeleine is no doubt watching over you."

"Lets hope so," Marjorie sighed and raised her bottle to toast her companions.

"Here's to getting Creighton out of jail."

George and Selina met her bottle with theirs, resulting in a resounding clink.

Marjorie took a swig of ginger beer and swallowed it. "It sounds like you and

Creighton's mother were very close."

"We were close friends," Selina confirmed. "She always teased and said that I was a better match for Richard than she was. I laughed at the time, but then, two years after Madeleine's death, there I was, in love with her widower."

"Have you ever told Creighton about your ginger beer 'get-togethers'? I'm sure he'd love to hear about them."

"No. Richard — Mr. Ashcroft — forbid us from talking about Mrs. Madeleine. It was tough on the boys, but especially Mr. Creighton. He was only nine years old and so lost after she died, poor lad. Mrs. Madeleine loved both of her boys, but she always had a special place in her heart for Mr. Creighton. They were of the same mind, those two."

"Creighton told me that they weren't permitted to speak of their mother after she died. I find it very strange," Marjorie mused. "I know Mr. Ashcroft's and Creighton's mother didn't get along well, but still . . ."

"That's what I needed to talk to you about," Selina stated as she tpped back her head and drank the rest of her ginger beer. "I need to tell you the reason Richard did not want to speak of his wife."

"Do you want me to leave?" George asked

as he hovered over his seat.

"Ye—" Selina started, and then changed her mind. "No. You may not know all there is to know about the world, but you're not a little boy. I don't want there to be any secrets on this island any longer."

"I'd like that," George beamed and sat back in his chair.

"Not so fast. You may not have to leave, but you can get us more ginger beer," Selina instructed as she reciprocated the smile.

George pulled a face and ran off toward the icebox.

"So," Selina prefaced, "where was I? Oh, yes. Last night, when Mr. Creighton argued with his father, he accused him of killing Mrs. Madeleine. Did he tell you what he meant?"

"Yes," Marjorie answered. "The night before his mother died, Creighton overheard his parents arguing. Apparently his father confessed to having an affair. Well, in truth, he more than confessed — he recounted every last detail."

George, in the meantime, returned with three new bottles, all the while giving Marjorie his rapt attention.

"George, my love," Selina snapped her son from his reverie. "Have you been drinking my ginger beer?"

George looked absently at the two bottles in his hands, each bearing a different amount of liquid. "Sorry," he muttered as he passed a bottle to his mother.

Selina accepted it with a smile and a good-humored wink in her son's direction.

Marjorie chuckled and then completed her story. "According to Creighton, Mrs. Madeleine was devastated at the news. She died the next morning."

"It's as I thought," Selina sighed and held her head. "I loved Mrs. Madeleine and, therefore, I've kept it a secret all these years, but I can't any longer. Mr. Creighton needs to find some peace with his father. The affair that Richard was describing wasn't his, it was hers."

"What!" Marjorie and George cried in unison.

"Before Mrs. Madeleine and Richard married, Mrs. Madeleine was seeing another young man. And she loved him, deeply. But he was poor and her family had lost their fortune in the last depression."

"So they pushed for her to marry someone else," Marjorie presumed.

"Yes," Selina confirmed. "Her family had a fine reputation, but no money. The Ashcrofts had money, but little in the way of reputation. It was a perfect match."

"Except that it didn't work," George stated.

"You took the words right out of my mouth," Marjorie laughed quietly.

"Mrs. Madeleine's parents got rid of the poor suitor."

"Naturally," Marjorie remarked.

"Some time later, two years or so after the Ashcrofts had married, the young man returned. He had made his fortune and asked Madeleine to leave Richard and run away with him. She should have taken the offer and run, but that wasn't Madeleine. She had taken a vow and she was determined to remain faithful to it, although she and the young man did write to each other on a regular basis. Long letters; beautiful letters. During one of our last ginger beer meetings, she let me read a few of those letters." Tears welled in Selina's eyes. "He had been with her the day she learned she had cancer, and had visited her at the house every afternoon since."

"Visited. Do you mean . . . ?" Marjorie asked.

"No," Selina stated emphatically. "Madeleine swore up and down that she had stayed truthful to her vows. I think even if she had wanted to, she was probably too sick anyway."

"If the relationship was platonic, why the big argument?" George asked. "And how did Mr. Ashcroft find out about the affair in the first place?"

"He found the letters," Selina explained. "And although Mrs. Madeleine maintained her innocence, Richard didn't believe her. Especially since the letters started shortly before Mr. Creighton came along —"

"He thought that Mr. Creighton was . . . ?" George uttered in disbelief.

"Richard could never understand the boy," Selina stated.

"Of course, how better to explain the differences than to claim he isn't yours?" Marjorie commented.

"Richard had been jealous of this other man from the outset," Selina resumed the story. "He knew that's where Madeleine's heart resided. The letters made him furious, but the situation did not come to a head until one afternoon. Richard came home early from work and found him there in the house on one of his afternoon visits. Richard had the man thrown out of the building, and he vowed to never let Madeleine see, speak, or write to him again. She never did."

"She died the next morning," Marjorie filled in the blanks.

Selina nodded.

The trio drank their ginger beers in silence.

"What am I supposed to do with this story?" Marjorie finally asked. "How is it going to help Creighton?"

"Mr. Creighton has spent his entire life believing that his mother had never known a day of happiness; that she never knew true love. And he's blamed all of that on his father. I'm not claiming that Richard's actions were entirely innocent during their marriage, but I do know that he loved Madeleine very much, and that he never stopped. I think he tried very hard at the beginning of the marriage to make her happy, to win her over. But he knew that she married him out duty to her family, and that he was her second choice for a husband. It's a difficult thing to love someone whose heart resides with someone else. Eventually, you give up on love altogether."

With a wry smile, Selina rose from her seat and quietly went about getting supper on the table.

Twenty-Four

It was going on nine o'clock by the time Marjorie, her stomach full of Selina's delicious chowder, departed from the cottage.

"I don't feel safe with you up in that big house tonight," Selina said worriedly. "Why don't you get your things and stay here?"

"You can have my room," George offered. "I'll sleep on the sofa."

"No, no," Marjorie argued. "I'll be all right at the house. I need to stay there to keep an eye on everyone. Besides, if anything happens, Inspector Nettles gave me this," she held up the shiny silver whistle.

"What are you supposed to do with that?" Selina asked skeptically. "Blow it in the murderer's ear?"

"It's a police whistle," Marjorie explained. "I blow on it and the Constable watching the pier will come to my rescue."

"I don't know about the Constable, but George and I will definitely come running."

207

Selina pulled a face, "Now I'm going to be awake all night, listening for the sound of a whistle."

"No, you won't. You're going to sleep well and get up tomorrow morning feeling better than you ever have." Marjorie reached her arms around the woman. "Thank you for dinner."

"You're welcome, child. And if you get frightened, please come here. It doesn't matter what time it is."

"I will," Marjorie assured her as she gave George a goodnight hug.

Meanwhile, Selina issued a warning to the black cat who, after devouring his dinner, had been lazing in the doorway all evening. "You look out for her, you hear? Otherwise it's no more fish chowder for you!"

The cat responded with a wide-mouthed "meow" before setting off on the path toward the house.

"Wait for me," Marjorie ordered and took off after him.

The cat stopped and watched with glowing eyes as she drew closer. Once she was within a few feet from him, he would take off again, only to stop a few yards down the path and monitor Marjorie's approach from behind a low shrub or a patch of tall grass. This game continued until they reached the rear entrance of the house.

Marjorie opened the back door and allowed her feline friend admittance before stepping inside. The comforting aromas of nutmeg and butter wafted through the hallway and enticed Marjorie to stick her head into the open kitchen door.

Mr. Miller sat at the long wooden table, eating a plate of starchy dumplings. Intrigued by the smell, the black cat jumped on the table to get a better look.

"Hello, Mrs. Ashcroft," Miller greeted. "And friend."

"Bad kitty," Marjorie rushed forward, scooped up the cat, and dropped him gently onto the kitchen floor. "I'm sorry, Mr. Miller. I wouldn't have let him in if I had known you were eating."

"That's all right, I had a dog like that back in Pennsylvania. Came in handy for the things I didn't like." He hiked a thumb to the frying pan on the stove. "Are you hungry? It's my mother's recipe; makes a bunch."

"No, thank you. I just had some fish chowder with the Pooleys."

"Selina and George?" Miller said doubtfully. "Was it wise to accept food from them?"

"No less wise than eating the food you

made," Marjorie stated matter-of-factly.

"Good point," he said with a smile.

Marjorie watched as Miller used his knife to push some dumplings onto the back of his fork. "Anything interesting happen around here while I was gone?"

"You mean more interesting than the murders? Or more interesting than your husband being arrested?"

"Now you're the one who's made a good point," she volleyed.

"Nothing happened and I'm sorry. Not about making a good point, but about your husband. For what it's worth, I don't think he did it." Miller dropped his voice to a whisper. "Between you and me, I think Edward's the culprit."

Marjorie sat opposite Miller and leaned in close. "Really? Why?"

"Because of the timing. By murdering Mr. Ashcroft when he did, he not only got rid of his arrogant father but he managed to make your husband look like the primary suspect. No one else here would be more interested in framing Creighton than his brother. What do you think?"

Miller pushed the last portion of dumplings onto his fork and carried them, carefully, to his mouth. Upon swallowing them, he picked up the plate and knife, and the napkin that had been resting on his lap, and brought them all to the sink.

"I have to admit, I'm at a total loss," she admitted. "Up until this afternoon, I thought Cassandra was the killer."

"She was pretty shady, wasn't she?" Miller washed his plate and the utensils with a soapy dishcloth and stacked them in the empty dish rack before drying his hands with a tea towel. "Well, I'm heading into the study for a drink. Would you care to join me?" he held his right arm aloft.

"I don't know," Marjorie said reluctantly.

"Oh, I didn't mean it that way," Miller clarified. "We wouldn't be alone. Griselda and Edward are there already. They've been 'unwinding' since five o'clock."

"It's been a long day," Marjorie noted. "I should probably get to bed."

"Just a quick drink? Something to help you sleep. You can't tell me that you're going to nod off the moment your head hits the pillow — not with your husband in jail and the real killer still on the loose."

Marjorie accepted the proffered arm. "You could have stopped at the part about my husband being in jail. You needn't have added the bit about the killer being on the loose."

Miller laughed as they made their way

down the hall, the small black cat following close at their heels. "There's safety in numbers. Since Cassandra's body was discovered, the three of us — four when George was here — have been trying to stick together."

They turned into the study to find Griselda, dressed to the nines in a red ruffle-fronted evening gown, draped across the settee, a martini glass in one hand and a cigarette in the other. "Marjorie!" she exclaimed upon seeing the blonde young woman standing in the doorway of the study. "Where have you been? Edward and I were positively in a panic over you!"

Edward, standing over the bar cart, shot a puzzled look in Griselda's direction before taking drink orders. "Marjorie. Miller. It's going to be a long night; what can I get you to drink?"

"I'll have a scotch and water," Miller requested.

"You want the same, Marjorie?" Edward asked as he poured a glass of scotch for Miller and another for himself.

"No, nothing quite that lethal," she replied.

"You should have a martini, darling," Griselda instructed. "They're good for what ails you."

There must have been some truth in that statement, for it appeared that Griselda wasn't feeling any pain at all. "I'll take your word on it," Marjorie responded before directing Edward. "I just want something to settle my nerves before I go to bed."

"Then brandy's the thing you want," Edward declared. He unstopped a glass decanter and poured some of the contents into a snifter.

"Brandy," Griselda repeated melodramatically. "My Richie had to have his brandy every night after dinner. Two glasses. No more, no less. Oh, Richie!" she wailed.

"This is her third crying jag tonight," Edward whispered to Marjorie as he passed her the snifter.

Marjorie suppressed a laugh. "Thank you," she said, swirling the contents of her glass.

"No need for that," Edward noted. "I could smell it the moment I opened the decanter; probably the heat. It's gone frightfully still outside, hasn't it?"

"Everything else around here is dying," Griselda noted. "Why should the breeze be any different?"

Miller took his drink from Edward and sat in one of the two wing chairs. "I think we're in for a storm," he opined.

Griselda swung her legs over the side of the settee in order to make a spot for Marjorie. "Swell. All we need is a Frankenstein monster and we'll have ourselves a genu-ine house of horrors."

Marjorie eased herself onto the cushion beside Griselda. As she did so, the cat jumped onto Marjorie's lap and began purring contentedly.

"Oh!" Griselda shrieked. "What is that?"

"Come now, Griselda," Edward joked. "If anyone should be able to recognize a cat, it's you."

Griselda glared at Edward. "I mean, what is it doing here?"

"I found him on the verandah outside our bedroom yesterday," Marjorie explained as she rubbed the cat's ears. "We've been friends ever since."

"You made friends with a black cat? Don't you know they're bad luck? Bad luck isn't exactly in short supply around here."

"According to Selina, it's worse luck to turn a black cat out of your home." Marjorie looked at the cat, "That's why you got fish chowder tonight, isn't it?"

Griselda bolted upright. "Selina made dinner? Why didn't I get any?"

"I told Selina to take the evening off," Edward answered. "After all she'd been through, I thought she could use the rest."

"It seems she didn't need the rest, if she was cooking for George and Marjorie and — and — a stray cat," Griselda said with venom. "She could have been cooking for us; I'm famished."

"Did it ever occur to you that you could make yourself something to eat?"

"I don't know how to cook!"

"You could always make a sandwich. There's roast beef in the icebox," Miller suggested.

"I don't even know where the icebox is, let alone the bread, and the knives and — and — oh, never mind," Griselda dismissed the idea. "I'm exhausted just thinking about it. Why do we even have servants if we don't let them do what they were hired to do?"

Edward laughed. "Only a few short hours ago you were accusing Selina and George of committing the murders. Now you want them to serve you supper."

"Excuse me if I'm dying from hunger and can't think straight. Besides, you're one to talk. You accused Marjorie of being the killer and here you are fixing her a brandy."

Marjorie looked angrily at her brother-in-law.

"I did not accuse Marjorie of being the killer," Edward contested. "I merely commented on the fact that my father was murdered on the same day she was introduced to the family. I found it an odd coincidence."

"That sounds like an indictment to me," Marjorie said.

"It wasn't," Edward maintained. "It isn't. It was an . . . observation, that's all."

"Yes, I've heard that observation before." Marjorie flashed a brilliant smile.

"Everyone seems to have an observation," Griselda slurred. "So what's your opinion, Mister . . . Mister Miller?"

"Me?" Miller asked in genuine surprise. "I think Edward here did it."

"I'm your suspect?" Edward responded ingenuously.

"Yes you are," Miller replied.

"Why?"

"You're just plain smug. And, if I may be bold, you drugged your wife. A man who's willing to do that to a lady cannot be trusted."

"Hmm," Edward responded appreciatively.

"Why didn't anyone pick me?" Griselda posed. "I could have murdered Richie and . . . and . . ."

"Cassandra?" Marjorie offered with a poorly disguised yawn.

"That's right," Griselda affirmed.

"If you want someone to concede that you could have returned early last night and snuck to the back of the house this afternoon, you've got it. Jackson, Nettles, and I all considered you a suspect." Marjorie yawned again.

Griselda sighed contentedly. "Yes, I am. I'm a suspect."

"For God's sake, go to bed," Edward urged.

"Well, I don't know about Griselda," Marjorie interjected as she took the black cat from her lap and placed him onto the cedar floorboards, "but I'm certainly ready."

"Now?" Griselda glanced at her watch. "It's only . . . nine-thirty. The party's just getting started."

"Maybe for you, but I —" Marjorie had risen to her feet, only to fall back onto the settee.

"Are you okay, Mrs. Ashcroft?" Miller asked.

"I — I just got a bit dizzy."

Edward rose from his spot in the wing chair and took hold of Marjorie's left arm. "You've had a long day. Let's get you to bed. Mr. Miller, will you give me a hand?"

Miller complied and took Marjorie's other arm.

"Wait," ordered Griselda. "You're not taking off with the only other woman in the house. And you're definitely not leaving me here by myself. I'm going with you!"

The trio, accompanied by the meowing black cat, assisted Marjorie up the cedar staircase and into her room. As Marjorie perched on the edge of the bed and unbuckled the ankle straps of her shoes, the cat leapt beside her and immediately began kneading the bedspread.

"She looks a bit pale. Perhaps you should stay with her," Miller suggested to Griselda.

"I'll change into my nightgown and be right back," Griselda took off down the hallway at breakneck speed.

Edward, meanwhile, had gone into the bathroom and retrieved a glass of water. "Here, drink this," he directed as he handed the glass to Marjorie.

"What is it?" Marjorie asked.

"It's water," Edward answered. "What did you think it was?"

"Nothing," Marjorie replied evasively.

"If I were trying to drug you, I wouldn't be so stupid as to do it with a glass of water or a snifter of brandy, with everyone watching," he insisted. "I'm sure this is just the day's events catching up with you."

"You're probably right," she admitted.

"I know I am," Edward replied. "Now get some sleep. If you or Griselda need anything, I'm right next door."

"Thank you, Edward," Marjorie answered as her brother-in-law disappeared into the hallway.

"I'd best be turning in as well," Miller announced. "If you need anything, I'm also next door — just on the other side."

"Thank you, Mr. Miller. Sleep well."

"You too," Miller said. He stepped out into the darkness of the hallway and closed the door behind him.

Marjorie staggered toward the dresser to find her nightgown, but the stagnant, moist air of the bedroom gave her pause. Determining that this was no night to be wearing silk, she slid out of her dress, discretely removed her brassiere from beneath her full slip, and lay on top of the covers listening to the sound of approaching footsteps.

The door opened to reveal Griselda, once again dressed to stun in a pink peignoir set trimmed with white feathers. "I'm so glad I'm bunking with you tonight. I feel a lot safer. Don't you?"

"Mmm," Marjorie grunted. At the moment, she felt little else but exhaustion — that is, until she heard a loud click emanating from the entrance. "Did you just lock the door?"

"Yes. You don't want the murderer to come in and kill us in our sleep do you?"

Marjorie motioned to the floor-to-ceiling windows, all of which were open. "The verandah wraps around the house, Griselda. And all the upstairs bedrooms have windows."

Griselda's face registered panic. "Oh, I didn't think of that! Should I close and bolt the windows?"

"Only if you want to know what the last moments of a clam's life feel like," Marjorie said groggily.

"Huh?"

"It's already over eighty degrees in here. If you shut the windows, we'll steam to death."

"But . . ." Griselda started.

"But what?" Marjorie asked.

"What about the murderer?"

"I'll take my chances," Marjorie replied as she clutched the police whistle tied loosely around her neck.

Griselda unlocked the door and removed the dressing gown portion of her peignoir before climbing into bed beside Marjorie. "This reminds me," she reminisced as she turned off the beside lamp, "of when I was a kid."

Marjorie sighed in annoyance.

"My sister and I shared a bed growing up. I got so used to it that I thought I'd never be able to sleep alone."

Despite her sleepiness, Griselda's statement elicited, in Marjorie's mind, at least one hundred different witty comebacks. She refrained from uttering any of them.

"It's only been the past couple of months that I've started to get used to it," Griselda went on. "I still didn't like it, mind you."

Marjorie sighed again in hopes that Griselda would take the hint.

"But Richie explained that he was working on something very important and that nighttime was the best time . . ."

It was becoming increasingly obvious that audience participation was not an essential element in Griselda's stories. However, it was becoming even more apparent that Marjorie's tired brain had no problem whatsoever in treating Griselda's nasal cadence as background noise. So adept were her gray cells at filtering out the nonsense proliferating Griselda's narrative that by the end of the story, Marjorie could remember only a few choice phrases before surrendering completely to the oblivion of slumber:

"Airplane plans . . . fewer interruptions . . . privacy . . . other hands . . ."

TWENTY-FIVE

Marjorie awoke the next day to find her bedroom both brighter and warmer than usual.

"Thank goodness you're awake," came a voice from the other side of the room.

Marjorie looked up to find, not Griselda, but Selina Pooley, seated on the stool that accompanied the nearby vanity table. Marjorie endeavored to pull herself up on one elbow, but the pounding pain in her temple forced her head back onto the pillow. "Selina?" she said questioningly. "What are you . . . ? What happened?"

The housekeeper moved to the edge of the bed and sat down. "Shh, settle down now, Miss Marjorie. You've just been sleeping, that's all."

"What time is it?"

"It's four o'clock."

"I've slept all day? Oh no! Creighton's hearing!" Marjorie bolted upright.

"Now don't you worry about that, Mrs. Marjorie," Selina assured. "Mr. Edward went in your place."

"He did?"

Selina poured a glass of water from the pitcher on Marjorie's bedside table and passed it to her. "It's a miracle, I know."

"Then Creighton's home?"

"No, child, not yet. Mr. Edward said he had to move some accounts around first. He's in Hamilton right now, trying to get it done."

"That's very kind of him," Marjorie noted. "If I can prove that Creighton isn't the murderer, he'll get his money back."

"You're not doing any of that detective work now, Miss Marjorie. Not until you're feeling better," Selina warned. "You were in an awful way this morning."

"Yes, I remember it started last night in the study. It came on so suddenly . . . Edward and Mr. Miller helped me upstairs, and Griselda stayed here, in my room."

Selina nodded. "You gave Mrs. Griselda quite a scare this morning. When she first tried to wake you, you didn't move. She came running downstairs in a panic. She thought you were dead."

"I must have been out cold," Marjorie remarked.

"You were," Selina answered. "She was beside herself, crying. Mr. Edward had gone with one of the constables to the hearing, so Mr. Miller went back upstairs with her to check on you. That's when you started talking gibberish. They couldn't make sense of anything you were saying."

"Almost like I had a fever . . ." Marjorie thought aloud.

"That's right. It was like what I had after finding Mr. Ashcroft in that trunk. I know the doctor gave me something to calm my nerves, but even before that, all I wanted to do was sleep. George blamed it on the brandy Mr. Creighton gave me but —"

"The brandy!" Marjorie exclaimed. She sprung from the bed and rummaged through the closet for something to throw on over her full slip. "Is Sergeant Jackson or Inspector Nettles here?"

"They were when I came up to sit with you. I don't know if they're still around; they had said they were going to make it an early day."

Marjorie pulled a green, flutter-sleeved day dress from its hanger, stepped into it, and pulled it up over her shoulders. Once Selina zipped the back of the dress, a barefoot Marjorie sprinted into the hallway and down the cedar staircase. Through the

224

windows that flanked either side of the heavy front door, she could see the figures of Jackson and Nettles walking down the white gravel path to the cove beyond.

Marjorie flung the front door open. "Wait!" she called.

The men continued on their way.

Realizing they hadn't heard her, she reached around her neck for the police whistle, but it wasn't there. *It must have fallen off while I was sleeping,* Marjorie thought to herself. "Wait!" she shouted again before taking off down the gravel path after the policemen.

"Ah, look, Nettles," Jackson teased once Marjorie was within earshot. "If it isn't Sleeping Beauty."

"I suppose that whistle worked," Nettles joked.

"Hmm?" Marjorie replied, her face a question.

"I gave you the whistle to help you rest easier," Nettles explained.

"Yes, you did, didn't you?" Marjorie answered distractedly. "That's actually the reason I followed you out here. You need to test the brandy."

"I'd love to," Jackson rejoined, "but we're on duty."

"No, not *taste* it, *test* it. Take it back to

Hamilton with you, because that's what put me to sleep last night and kept me asleep all this morning and afternoon."

"And what are we supposed to test the brandy for?"

"Seconal," she responded drily.

"Ah yes, the 'missing' Seconal tablets," Jackson said. "I was wondering where they might turn up. I had no idea you'd claim they were put into your glass of brandy."

"They weren't put in my glass, they were added to the decanter. And they didn't just turn up; they've been there all along. That's why it took so long for Selina to wake up yesterday and why Creighton was sound asleep in the cottage yesterday afternoon: they both drank the brandy."

"Mrs. Ashcroft," Jackson argued, "the past couple of days have been difficult for everyone. If Selina and your husband were tired, it's most likely due to the strain of the situation."

"And what about me?" she challenged. "I know what I experienced and it wasn't emotional strain. I felt like I had been drugged."

"Mmm. Did you drink anything else last night? Eat anything?"

"I had fish chowder with Selina and George."

226

"With rum in it?"

"Well, yes," she reluctantly replied.

"Well, there you go," Jackson declared. "You can't go mixing different types of spirits like that, Mrs. Ashcroft."

"Mixing spirits? I had a tablespoon of rum and a snifter of brandy."

"You never know. That rum can sneak up on you."

"If what I suffered were the effects of a tablespoon of rum, then I don't know why hospitals waste their time with ether! It was the brandy, I tell you." She suddenly recalled the previous night's events. "Look, if you don't believe me, ask Edward. He opened the decanter. He'll tell you it had an usually strong aroma."

Jackson's eyes narrowed. "All right, let's assume for a moment that your theory is correct. What's the motive?"

"Motive?"

"Yes. Why would someone put Seconal in the brandy?"

Marjorie shook her head slowly, until an idea suddenly burst forth. "Wait one minute! Griselda said that Mr. Ashcroft drank brandy — two glasses — after dinner every night."

"So?" Jackson prodded.

"So, that's a habit anyone in the house

would have noticed. It makes me wonder if the killer didn't try to take advantage of it."

"By putting Seconal in the brandy?" Nettles guessed.

"Yes," Marjorie stated. "It would have been easier to slip the Seconal into the decanter without being seen than to drug Ashcroft's glass."

"If drugged brandy was meant for Ashcroft, why is it still there?" Nettles asked.

"The killer didn't have the opportunity to get rid of it. We were in the study all day yesterday," Marjorie explained. "Besides, you never know when that sort of thing might come in handy. Especially since the source of the Seconal is in Hamilton Hospital."

"You're forgetting something, aren't you? The murderer put your father-in-law to sleep permanently," Jackson pointed out. "There was little need to use barbiturates."

"The Sergeant's right," Nettles agreed. "A bronze statue over the head is much more effective than sleeping pills."

"Granted, but what if murder wasn't the killer's original intent? What if the plan was to drug Ashcroft with the Seconal?" Marjorie hypothesized. "And what if somehow, somewhere along the line, something went wrong with that plan? Inspector Nettles, you and I were both of the opinion that Cassandra's death was an act of desperation."

Nettles nodded. "Broad daylight with scads of policemen around? I'd say so."

"Sounds about right to me," Jackson weighed in.

"Well, what if murdering Ashcroft was also a last resort?"

Jackson chuckled. "Of course it was a last resort. This was a crime of passion, wasn't it? Whoever murdered Ashcroft did so because Ashcroft was, for lack of a better description, a louse and a bully. The killer had had his fill of Ashcroft's behavior and clocked him one on the back of the head. It certainly wasn't premeditated."

"That's right!" Marjorie said excitedly. "The murder *wasn't* premeditated, but something else *was*. Think about it: the elaborate scheme to get Ashcroft here, the confirmation telegram, and the threatening note. Something else had to be going on."

"I think you're reaching," Jackson judged.

"And I think you're not reaching enough," Marjorie countered. "You've had my husband in custody for twenty-four hours now and you're still completely unwilling to admit that you've made a mistake."

"Because I have no reason, apart from your theories, to even consider the possibil-

229

ity that someone else committed the murders. Your husband had the most to gain from Mr. Ashcroft's death. In fact, he was the only person with anything to gain financially. Case closed."

"But no one — not even Creighton — knew who was named in that will. Sure, Edward assumed that it was Creighton, but it was anyone's guess as to whether or not that assumption was correct. It was anyone's guess, for that matter, as to whether the Old Man had even changed his will. He might have been bluffing."

"But he wasn't bluffing, was he?"

"No one knew that at the time," Marjorie shouted. "Ashcroft was murdered because something he did that night threw a wrench into someone's plans — and I don't mean financial plans. To murder someone on the off chance that you've been written into, or out of, their will, simply doesn't wash."

"And what about you, Mrs. Ashcroft?" Jackson said smugly. "Have you washed?"

"What? What in heaven's name are you talking about?"

"I'm talking about you, Mrs. Ashcroft, and the fact that you only just woke up a short time ago and immediately came out here firing off all sorts of crazy ideas. Here's what I suggest: Nettles and I return to Hamilton;

230

I meet my wife for supper as I promised; and you, Mrs. Ashcroft, have a long bath and something to eat and give serious thought to all you've suggested today."

"You needn't be condescending," Marjorie chided.

"I'm not being condescending, Mrs. Ashcroft. If you come up with anything new, don't hesitate to call me. Oh, wait," Jackson feigned ignorance, "you don't have a phone here, do you? I guess anything else will have to wait until I see you in the morning."

"Funny," Marjorie remarked. "Very funny."

"Yes, I am. That's why Mrs. Jackson has requested that I be home in time for supper," the Sergeant smiled and tipped his hat. "And cheer up. Maybe you'll be lucky and your brother-in-law will bail him out this evening." He took off down the path, whistling happily.

"Do you have the decanter?" Nettles asked quietly.

Marjorie nodded and then bolted into the house. She returned a few seconds later, the decanter tucked under one arm. "Oh, I forgot to ask. Did Detective Jameson call today?"

"No, but we haven't been at the station since this morning. If he left a message, I'll send it over with Constable Smith. He's on duty again tonight; he'll be here by six."

"I'll keep an eye out for him."

Nettles looked around suspiciously. "Keep an eye out for yourself while you're at it. If this brandy has been tampered with, the perpetrator is going to notice when it goes missing. You still have your whistle?"

"Yes, it's, uh, upstairs," Marjorie replied.

"Good girl. Use it if you need it." Nettles took the decanter from her hand and, with a smile and a wink, followed the Sergeant to the cove.

Marjorie turned on one heel and went back into the house. Despite the patronizing manner in which it was suggested, she had to admit that the idea of relaxing in a tub was an extremely appealing one.

As Marjorie made her way toward the staircase, she was startled by the sound of a voice resonating through the high-ceilinged entryway. "Mrs. Ashcroft," Miller greeted. "Good to see you up and about."

"Thank you, Mr. Miller. It's good to be back . . . umm . . . amongst the living."

"We were all very worried about you. Griselda had you as murdered in your sleep. I don't think she realized that it wouldn't have looked very good for her if you had been," Miller laughed.

"No it wouldn't have, would it?" Marjorie chuckled.

"Say," Miller segued, "I was in the office, looking for a postage stamp, and couldn't help but notice you talking to Sergeant Jackson and Inspector Nettles. Have they left for the day?"

"Yes. They'll be back tomorrow."

"Ah," he replied. "I'm sorry if it seems like I was eavesdropping. I wasn't, I assure you. It's the location of that office, between the view of the front lawn and the view of the front door, you can see everyone coming and going."

"It is quite the vantage point," Marjorie remarked.

Miller nodded. "Well, I just wanted to let you know I'm glad you're all right. I won't keep you. I know you were on your way upstairs."

"Yes, I'm in rather dire need of a bath."

"Sounds like just the thing. Will you be down for dinner? Selina's back on duty tonight."

"Griselda will be happy to hear that," Marjorie remarked. "Yes, I'll be down for dinner. Eight o'clock?"

"That's right," Miller confirmed. "I'll see you then." He nodded his goodbye and went into the study.

With a smile, Marjorie turned and began her ascent up the wide, cypress staircase. Suddenly, she stopped, her foot poised over the first step. The smile washed away from Marjorie's face as a vague memory fought its way into her consciousness and then, before it could be identified, retreated back into the darkness.

Marjorie put her foot down onto the tread and continued up the stairs, all the while taking a mental inventory of her conversation with Miller. What was said to trigger that memory? And, more importantly, did the recollection condemn Miller? Or did it point the finger at someone else?

TWENTY-SIX

Marjorie lowered herself slowly into the sudsy water, drew a deep breath, and attempted to quiet the various thoughts and ideas racing through her head.

Whereas showering was a completely utilitarian exercise, bathing, for Marjorie, was a meditative activity. An hour spent splashing, lathering, and rinsing not only cleansed dirt and perspiration from the body, but purified her mind of distractions, thus providing Marjorie with a renewed and refined focus on the problem at hand. Indeed, a good long soak in a warm tub had helped her work through many of the more difficult plot lines in her novels.

The puzzle which she currently faced, however, was much more complicated. Unlike her novels, the characters and dialogue of this particular drama were not of her creation, making the dénouement a potentially tragic one for all involved.

Marjorie leaned against the high back of the claw-foot tub, closed her eyes, and reviewed the facts of the case.

First, there was the body. Mr. Ashcroft had been struck on the back of the head with a blunt object — in this case, the bronze statuette from the downstairs hallway. Marjorie shook her head slowly; it was a risky, messy murder that couldn't have been premeditated. Why couldn't Jackson see, as she did, that the whole scenario reeked of desperation?

Mr. Ashcroft was a tall man with a sturdy build, and, by all appearances, was in good health. There had to be an easier, more foolproof way of killing him than bashing his brains in with a household curio. Likewise, the murderer might have been seen by the other eight people in the house or even by Ashcroft himself. One shout from the Old Man and the entire game would have been over, unless . . .

The brandy.

Marjorie took a bar of soap from the adjacent wire rack and began lathering her arms and legs absently. If Ashcroft drank the brandy (which Marjorie still maintained contained the missing Seconal tablets), he would have been asleep or, at the very least, too groggy to notice or fight his assailant.

But, as Jackson pointed out, why drug a man only to cosh him over the head later? Why not slip poison, rather than Seconal, into the brandy, and get the job over with?

Because, she argued with Jackson and now herself, the killer didn't intend to be a killer. At that point, he or she was getting Ashcroft out of the way temporarily. He or she was simply buying time.

Buying time, she turned the phrase over in her mind. Buying time seemed to be a recurring theme in this case: first the phony appointment meant to lure the Ashcrofts out of New York and to Bermuda, then the counterfeit confirmation designed to get Mr. Ashcroft and possibly Mr. Miller away from Black Island, and, finally, the Seconal-laced brandy, administered to Ashcroft to ensure his complete withdrawal from the world at large.

Even the concealment of the body in the chest, aside from implicating Creighton, could be construed as an attempt to delay the discovery of Mr. Ashcroft's murder. Selina, when questioned, claimed that the lid was closed when she entered the dining room that morning. If the chest had been watertight, Mr. Ashcroft's body may not have been uncovered until Marjorie and Creighton crated the piece for delivery to the United States, possibly even later.

But why? Why so much subterfuge and misdirection? The reasons for hiding the body were obvious. Doing so made it tougher for the police to pinpoint the time of death, thus giving the killer an opportunity to establish an alibi. Moreover, if the chest containing Mr. Ashcroft had actually been crated and shipped, the resulting murder investigation would have been a logistical, as well as bureaucratic, nightmare.

What Marjorie didn't understand was how it might behoove anyone to drug Mr. Ashcroft, or to send him on a wild goose chase. Why did they need him out of the house, or out of their hair, so badly? What was the plan —

Marjorie stopped in mid-thought and let the bar of soap slip through her fingers. She had listened to enough of Griselda's nattering the previous night to understand that Mr. Ashcroft had been working on a new airplane, the design for which was so innovative that Ashcroft would only view the plans late at night and in the security of his own home. Marjorie had also read enough about the situation in Europe (namely the recent German rearmament and Italy's potential invasion of Ethiopia) to realize how valuable the new design would be to certain foreign powers, and just how lucrative those plans would be for whoever possessed them.

Suddenly it all became clear. Even the Bermuda locale had been handpicked in order to take advantage of the regatta, an event attended by boating enthusiasts and dignitaries from around the world. If one were to be seen speaking with a foreign representative on the streets of Hamilton, who would be the wiser?

What wasn't clear, however, was the identity of the person behind the plot. Edward, as second in command, was more than likely aware of the project and its potential worth on the international market; he was also the only person to have seen the telegram confirming the spurious appointment. Did he scheme to resell the plans in a last-ditch attempt to purchase his independence?

And what about Pru? It wasn't unreasonable to think that Edward could have mentioned the new project to his wife or that she might have overheard it being discussed around the dinner table. Between the miscarriage, the Seconal, and now the Benzedrine she was certainly desperate enough to try anything to get away from her father-in-law's watchful eye. Yet, if George's account was accurate, Pru was en route to the hospital when Cassandra was murdered. Could they have worked together to commit the crimes? If so, it would shed new light on Pru's reluctance to speak with the police.

As Mr. Ashcroft's secretary, Mr. Miller was high on the list of those who knew about the new airplane design. The only problem was that he had been dispatched, along with Ashcroft, to the now notorious Hamilton appointment, which indicated to Marjorie that someone wanted both of them away from the house and, more specifically, the office.

After having given the story to Marjorie, there was no way that Griselda could refute her knowledge of the drawings. Was Griselda aware that the sale of those plans could have kept her and her beloved Benny safe and warm in their New Jersey love nest for many years to come? If so, why divulge any of it to Marjorie — a woman she knew had been working with the police? Or was the unseen Benny the brains of the operation, and had Griselda — never-too-blonde, never-too-thin, never-too-tanned Griselda — simply said too much in an effort to satiate her constant need for attention?

Even George and Selina could not be

completely exonerated. When Ashcroft offered George a position as property manager, he might have mentioned, or more likely bragged about, his new design. If Ashcroft had disclosed the existence of those plans to George, the boy would have, undoubtedly, shared the information with his mother. Although Marjorie desperately hoped that the Pooleys were innocent, she couldn't blame them if they had sought to attain George's tuition money through alternate methods.

Finally, what was Cassandra's role in this mystery? Had she witnessed the murder and decided to blackmail the killer? Or had she also been aware of the existence of the plans and tried to hold out for a share of the sale?

Marjorie drained the tub, stood up and switched on the shower. *She had to talk to the police,* she thought as she rinsed the soap from her limbs and torso. *Who was she kidding? Jackson wouldn't believe a word of any of this.* Marjorie thrust her head under the warm water. *No, before she spoke to anyone she needed proof.*

She shut the water off and pushed her wet hair away from her face. She needed to find those plans, but where could she look that the killer hadn't already checked? And what if she was caught during her search? She might suffer the same fate as Ashcroft and Cassandra.

As she stepped out of the tub and onto the plush mat, a thought occurred to Marjorie. *The police whistle. It might not help her fight off an attacker, but it would attract the attention of everyone on the island.*

She wrapped a towel around her wet head, donned her robe, and rushed into the bedroom, only to be enwrapped by a pair of sinuous orangey-brown arms.

"Marjorie!" Griselda screeched. "Selina told me you were awake. Oh, thank goodness. We were both so worried about you."

Marjorie returned the embrace. "Thanks Griselda."

Griselda pulled back and looked Marjorie in the eyes. "I . . . I thought you were dead. I thought someone came in here in the middle of the night and killed you."

"No, I was just in a deep sleep."

"It's this heat and humidity," Griselda clicked her tongue and flopped her lithe, swimsuit-clad figure onto the bed. "I bet you had that sleeping sickness disease. We should get some sort of netting on these canopies to keep the bugs out."

"There are no mosquitoes in Bermuda," Marjorie stated as she patted the bedspread around Griselda for a sign of something hidden beneath the covers. "Say, did you happen to notice the whistle I was wearing around my neck last night?"

"What, that big shiny metal thing? That was a whistle?"

"A police whistle, yes." She got down on all fours and checked under the bed. "Do you recall if I was still wearing it this morning?"

Griselda cast her eyes heavenward. "Let's see . . . I woke up this morning because that cat creature of yours was biting my toes. He was sinking his teeth into me like a furry little Bela Lugosi. He wanted my blood, I swear! Anyway, I tried to wake you so you could pull the demon off of me, but you wouldn't budge. I rolled you over onto your back because you were on your side, facing the window, and . . ."

"And?" Marjorie urged.

"And . . . yes, you were still wearing it."

"Then where did it go?" Marjorie wondered aloud.

"It probably fell off while you were sleeping. Selina made the bed, maybe she knows where it is," Griselda suggested.

"Maybe, but she knew Inspector Nettles gave it to me as . . ." Marjorie's voice trailed off as she realized the importance of her words. Selina knew about the police whistle.

Did she put it in her pocket for safekeeping until she could return it to Marjorie? Or did she take it to ensure that Marjorie couldn't summon Officer Smith if or when she needed help?

For that matter, how could Marjorie be certain that Griselda was even telling the truth in the first place? Given how soundly Marjorie had slept, it would have been easy for Griselda to remove the string from around Marjorie's neck and then feign innocence.

"What's wrong?" Griselda asked, prompted by Marjorie's extended period of silence.

"Nothing," Marjorie replied. Although she was aware of the need to consider everyone a suspect, she also knew that overanalyzing what was, most likely, an innocuous mix-up, was not only bad for her nerves, but created in those around her a sense of wariness. "I was just thinking of what I would have done if I had found it. I probably would have put it on the night table or the dresser. After all, isn't that what Selina does with your things?"

Griselda stretched out on her stomach and rested her head on her arms. "I don't know, she never made up our room; Richie always did. Even at home, he never let the servants near the bedroom. It was his pet peeve."

Marjorie paused and stared past Griselda. Could the answer be that simple? Did Ashcroft keep the plans in his bedroom? Creighton said that his father used to "hide away" important documents instead of putting them in the safe. Where better to keep them than close at hand?

The bedroom, Marjorie determined, would be the first place she'd search once everyone had gone to bed. But first, she had to ensure that Griselda wouldn't be there.

"I'll ask Selina about the whistle when we go downstairs for dinner," Marjorie announced. "Speaking of dinner," she announced casually, "when are you getting ready? If we're going to be bunking together, we'll need to schedule our bathroom and mirror time."

"You want me to stay with you?" Griselda asked hopefully.

"Of course. Why not?"

"Well, last night, you seemed kinda irritated."

"I was tired and cranky, that's all," Marjorie waved her hand dismissively. "Now that I'm feeling better, I think it's a great idea. With Edward's and Miller's rooms on either side of mine, I know I'd feel safer if I didn't have to sleep alone."

Griselda rolled onto her side and propped herself up on one elbow. "Oh, I know! Now that you've reminded me about the verandah, I don't think I'd sleep a wink by myself. I'd be staring at the windows all night." She frowned. "Oh, wait . . . Creighton's coming back tonight, isn't he?"

"I don't know. Last thing I heard is that Edward had to rearrange some of his accounts, but neither of them have come back yet." Marjorie went to the dresser and selected some clean undergarments. "However, even if Creighton comes back tonight, I still think you should stay. We're the only women left in the main house; we need to stick together."

"But Creighton," Griselda argued, "how will he feel? It is your honeymoon after all."

"Some honeymoon: two dead bodies and a husband in jail." Marjorie shook her head and then made her way to the closet. "Creighton is a gentleman. He wouldn't want you staying by yourself any more than I do. When he gets back, he can take your room, while you stay here."

Marjorie gave herself a mental pat on the back for that little flourish. If tonight's search didn't pan out, Creighton's access to that bedroom might come in handy.

With a high-pitched squeal, Griselda

bounded from the bed and nearly tackled Marjorie. "Oh, thank you! I'm glad you said something because I really wasn't looking forward to going back to my room tonight."

It was not the reaction Marjorie had anticipated, but it was quite revealing. If Griselda had been behind the plot to steal the drawings, the last thing she would want to do is give up her room and the freedom to search the house after hours.

"Besides," Griselda continued, "I had fun last night."

"You did?"

"Uh huh. My sister moved out west a few years back and I don't have any girlfriends. Pru lives with us but," Griselda pulled a face. "The only people I've had to talk to are Richie and Benny, so it was nice to have a good long talk with a woman for a change."

Marjorie scoured her memory for an indication of when this "talk" may have occurred. "I don't think I said much. Did I?"

"No, but you're a terrific listener. Thanks, it was just what I needed!"

"You're welcome. I enjoyed it too . . . despite the fact that I was unconscious." Marjorie smiled politely. "Listen, why don't you go get your dress and the other stuff you'll need and we'll get ready for dinner."

Griselda looked at her watch. "We still have plenty of time."

"Yes, but it's a beautiful day — much more comfortable than yesterday — and I want to enjoy it."

"Ooh! We can sit outside and watch the boats in Hamilton Harbor," Griselda proposed. "I'll make Manhattans."

"Sure," Marjorie agreed with a shrug before dispatching Griselda.

There was a lot of time to kill before nightfall, Marjorie thought. *Too much time.*

Twenty-Seven

Marjorie, dressed in a light blue chiffon evening dress, and Griselda, in a bright yellow crepe de chine hostess gown, sat on a pair of white wrought-iron garden benches set upon the front lawn of the Black Island residence, sipping Manhattans from round-based cocktail glasses.

"I feel like I'm in *The Great Gatsby*," Griselda declared. "What with the view of the harbor and the docks and the two of us out here in our formal dresses, drinking cocktails."

"You read *The Great Gatsby*?" Marjorie asked in surprise.

"Yeah, you think I only read movie star magazines? I read romances, too and I liked *Gatsby*. I liked *Love on the Adriatic* and *The Longshore Girl* better, but *Gatsby* was okay. I could understand Daisy Buchanan, loving one man but marrying the man who could give her a better life."

"My detective hat is off," Marjorie prefaced, "So, anything you say is strictly in confidence, but you did marry Mr. Ashcroft for his money, didn't you?"

"Honestly? I loved Richie; I still do. He treated me better than any man I've ever been with and I'm going to miss him something terrible. But, the truth is, I was never 'in love' with him. It's probably just as well I wasn't, otherwise the things he said and did would have hurt me a lot more." Griselda took a swig of her Manhattan. "So, to answer your question, no I didn't marry Richie for the money. But I don't know if I would have married him without it. I know that sounds awful, but you, of all people, should know what I mean."

"Me?" Marjorie questioned.

"I know you love Creighton. And God knows you wouldn't be trying to clear his name if you weren't 'in love' with him too," Griselda asserted. "But you can't say that the money isn't the icing on the cake."

"Well, I make money from my books," Marjorie begged the question, "so I've had it better than a lot of other people."

"Yeah, I know, I've made my own money too, but not the kind of money the Ashcrofts have."

Marjorie sipped her Manhattan silently.

"Before I worked as a secretary, I was a seamstress, you know," Griselda said as she stood up and spun around. "I made this dress."

"Really?" Marjorie took the hem of Griselda's gown in her hands. Despite the hideous color, Marjorie had to admit that it was a piece of quality workmanship. "Your stitches are perfect. I had no idea . . . I thought you had always been a secretary."

"God, no," Griselda laughed and sat back down on the bench. "I only got the job with Richie because my sister was his previous secretary. She was leaving to get married and I was taking in mending and doing dress alterations, but it wasn't going to be enough once my sister moved out. So she recommended to Richie that I take her place."

"That worked out well," Marjorie remarked.

"Not right away. I'd never been trained to use a typewriter or anything like that. My father was a tailor and my mother was a seamstress. They had a little shop in Passaic — not anything big, but they did a good business. From early on, I was trained to help with the mending and eventually became a full-fledged seamstress. Not as good as Mama, though. When we'd do weddings, Mama always did the bride's gown while I did the bridesmaids," Griselda smiled and shook her head. "My sister could never get the hang of sewing, poor thing, so she wound up taking care of the office and the bills."

"Well, it was good preparation for her secretarial work," Marjorie commented.

Griselda nodded and poured the remainder of the contents of the cocktail shaker into their now-empty glasses. "I wish she hadn't needed it. But after the crash, people weren't having their dresses and suits made any longer; they were buying them off the rack — even brides. We still had the occasional batch of mending or an alteration to do, but folks learned pretty quickly how to fix their clothes themselves. The shop closed a year later, and with it, my father's dream. He died a few months later, followed shortly by my mother."

"I'm sorry," Marjorie said, sympathetically.

"Thanks. What hurts most is that, if I had the money I have now back then, I could have saved the business and my parents might still be alive. I hated being poor. I hated pinching every penny. But the worst part of not having money is not being able to help the people you care about. I never want to be in that spot again," Griselda vowed.

Marjorie thought of her own father. If she had met Creighton just a year or two earlier, might she have been able to pay for a treatment that would have prolonged her father's life? It was a painful question, but at the moment, she had more pressing issues to consider. Specifically, had Griselda's fear of poverty spurred her to steal the plans for the new aircraft?

A couple of days, even a few hours, earlier, Marjorie might have dismissed the idea outright, citing Griselda's penchant for movie magazines and brightly colored, somewhat revealing clothing as visible proof of her academic shortcomings. Their current conversation, although failing to establish Griselda as an intellectual, revealed that the woman was far shrewder and far more determined to succeed than anyone might have first imagined.

"Good evening, ladies," the voice of Mr. Miller interrupted Marjorie's musings. "Is this soiree for women only?"

"Mr. Miller," Marjorie replied. "Please join us."

"Yeah, pull up a chair," Griselda rejoined.

"Thank you." Miller lifted the matching wrought-iron chair from its location a few feet away and positioned it between the two benches. "Say, I hope you ladies don't mind, but I took the liberty of asking Selina and George to serve us dinner outdoors this evening. I thought we could enjoy the cooler air and watch the boats as they arrive in Hamilton for the regatta tomorrow."

"What a nice idea," Marjorie stated.

"Sounds good to me," Griselda chimed in.

"And after dinner," Miller continued, "when it's dark, Constable Worth told me there's going to be fireworks. To kick off the start of the festivities."

"Oh, I love fireworks!" Griselda exclaimed as she picked up the empty cocktail shaker. "Marjorie, hon, your glass is empty. Should I mix us up another round?"

Marjorie picked up her glass and stared at it indecisively. There were still quite a few hours left before she would need to practise her sleuthing skills. "Sure. Why not?" she finally consented.

Griselda smiled and nodded. "Mr. Miller, you look thirsty. How about a Manhattan?"

"When you ask that nicely, how can I resist? Do you need a hand?" he offered.

"Are you kidding? I could mix Manhattans in my sleep," Griselda quipped before setting off toward the house to refill the shaker.

"Just between us," Miller confessed quietly to Marjorie, "I didn't want to eat in the dining room tonight. It seemed . . ."

"Macabre?" Marjorie filled in the blank.

"Yes. I wasn't sure how Mrs. Ashcroft was going to take it either. She can be quite . . . emotional . . . at times."

"That's a polite way of putting it," Marjorie chuckled.

"Oh? She didn't go on another crying jag last night, did she? She was supposed to be keeping an eye on you."

"No, nothing like that. Just a healthy dose of nattering."

"I'm sorry I suggested she stay with you. I hope she didn't keep you awake," Miller said sincerely.

"Mr. Miller," Marjorie replied, "Hannibal could have marched his elephants through my bedroom last night and I wouldn't have noticed."

Miller laughed out loud. "You're feeling better now, I hope," he asked, his voice tinged with genuine concern. "Because when I met you on the stairs, you seemed rather anxious."

"Much better, thanks. The bath did wonders."

"Yes it did," Miller agreed. "You look quite lovely tonight. If I may be so bold, your husband is a lucky man."

Marjorie felt the color rise in her cheeks. "Thank you," she murmured.

"I apologize if that was too forward," Miller excused. "I — I just happened to notice that you keep a careful eye on the harbor. Not on the boats arriving, but the boats leaving. You're waiting for Creighton, aren't you?"

"You're very observant, Mr. Miller," she said with a smile.

"Not really. I think I noticed it only because I wish I had someone waiting for me when I get home — someone like you."

"Come now," Marjorie coaxed. "There must be some girl back home who's caught your eye."

"There's plenty who've caught my eye," Miller chuckled. "The problem is catching theirs."

"I find it hard to believe that no one's even glanced in your direction."

"I don't know. Maybe they have and I haven't noticed. My work has occupied most of my time as of late." Miller frowned.

"I imagine it has," Marjorie said thoughtfully. *Was Miller speaking of his work with the demanding Mr. Ashcroft, or was he referring to the equally demanding, yet infinitely more profitable, task of stealing the drawings?*

Griselda had returned with the cocktail shaker and an extra glass for Miller. George, carrying the table that rounded out the patio set, followed several paces behind her.

"Here, let me give you a hand." Miller rose from his chair and assisted George in moving the table into place.

Selina appeared a few moments later with a stack of plates and napkins in one hand and a butcher paper–lined basket filled with golden brown pieces of dough in the other. "Shark fritters," she announced as she placed her cargo on the table.

"Shark?" Griselda screeched.

"My mother used to make fritters with potatoes," Miller remarked as he popped one in his mouth.

"Potatoes?" Selina said uncertainly.

"They were delicious, just like these," Miller assured, much to Selina's delight.

Marjorie tried one. The combination of fish and batter melted in her mouth. "Mmm! Selina, these are wonderful."

"Why, thank you."

Griselda, having listened to as much praise as she could stand, took a tentative bite of fritter. "Hmph, not bad," she allowed before polishing off the remainder.

"I feel badly about you and George having to bring everything out here," Marjorie said to Selina. "Is there anything I can help you with?"

"No, child. Cooking and serving are nothing — I enjoy them. And George can take care of everything else. But if I can think of anything, I'll give you a whistle."

"That reminds me, Selina, I can't find the whistle Inspector Nettles gave me. Did you happen to see it when you made the bed earlier today?"

"The one you were wearing around your neck? No, I haven't seen it since you showed it to me last night."

"That's strange," Marjorie commented. "I thought for certain it must have fallen off while I was sleeping."

"It probably came off when you went downstairs after Inspector Nettles and Sergeant Jackson. The way you were running, I wouldn't be surprised," Selina opined and then turned on one heel and headed back to the house.

Marjorie pulled a face. She supposed it was possible that the whistle had come loose during her frenzied sprint from the bedroom to the front door; however, she had been both up and down that flight of stairs since Nettles and Jacksons' departure and hadn't seen the whistle or the string. But, of course, she hadn't been looking for it either.

With a brief word to her companions, she journeyed back to the house to retrace her steps that afternoon. Scanning the ground as she walked, she followed the white gravel path to the front steps. Placing her foot on the bottom step, she looked up to see George gazing out the office window to the harbor beyond.

It was a shame, Marjorie thought, for a young man like George to be stuck on the island while his friends were undoubtedly enjoying the festivities in Hamilton. She recalled her younger years and the anticipation she and her friends felt as the school year ended and Independence Day drew near. There were dances and graduation parties and then the highlight of a young person's summer: the Ridgebury Fourth of July Picnic, complete with fireworks by the brook. It was during those fireworks, against the flickering lights and the deafening pops and crackles, that a fifteen-year-old Marjorie received her first kiss. Perhaps George had enjoyed a similar experience during the regatta fireworks. Perhaps there was even a girl with whom he had hoped to watch the fireworks tonight.

As if he could read her thoughts, George

turned his head toward Marjorie and issued a melancholy smile. Marjorie responded with a friendly wave, but it was too late; George had already retreated into the dark recesses of the Black Island house.

Marjorie continued up the front steps, but the image of George Pooley staring back at her from the office window stirred a memory within her. *That* was what had been bothering her ever since her conversation with Miller. The *vantage point.*

That single phrase unleashed a tidal wave of seemingly disparate images that all, somehow, clicked into place.

Marjorie felt a cold spot develop in her stomach. She now knew who committed the murders, but if she were correct, the killer's motive was more sinister than anything she had ever before encountered.

TWENTY-EIGHT

Her search for the whistle having yielded a solution to the case, but no whistle, Marjorie returned to the table just in time for dinner.

"Sweetie, your Manhattan was getting warm," Griselda greeted. "So I drank it. I hope you don't mind."

Marjorie laughed and grabbed Griselda's hand warmly as she passed behind her seat. "That's fine," she excused. "I think I'll drink something else with my meal."

"I pulled an excellent bottle of Gewürztraminer from the cellar," Miller stated. "Would you care to share it with me?"

Marjorie eyed the bottle suspiciously.

"It's still corked," Miller assured. "And if makes you feel better, you can pour your own glass."

"That would be lovely," she accepted as she sat down upon the bench she had previously occupied. "Not that I don't trust you —"

"But you don't trust me," Miller quipped.

"Oh, no," Marjorie argued, taking great pains not to protest too much.

"Don't worry, Mrs. Ashcroft. If the shoe were on the other foot, I'd be reluctant to let you pour as well."

"I wouldn't blame you, what with my being a mystery writer," Marjorie teased. It was imperative that she maintain a calm, relaxed, jovial façade. For, despite the unfortunate circumstances behind their island imprisonment, this was supposed to be a relaxing evening amongst friends; any indication of fear or anxiety might arouse suspicion.

Griselda stood up, the cocktail shaker in her hand. "Are you sure you wouldn't like a Manhattan to replace the one I drank? I'm making another batch."

"No, thank you, Griselda," Marjorie declined.

"Suit yourself," Griselda remarked as she half walked, half stumbled back to the house.

"The next one will make number six," Miller stated drily.

"She had three more while I was gone?" Marjorie questioned.

Miller nodded. "Two of her own and one of yours."

"And that shaker holds two or three more. Bringing the total to seven or eight . . . oh boy!"

"Uh huh, looks like another night of Griselda's carryings on."

"Maybe some food will sober her up," Marjorie said hopefully as she watched George approach, bearing a tray laden with three covered plates. "Last night she was drinking on an empty stomach."

"True," Miller allowed. "But tonight she started earlier and is drinking whiskey."

George distributed three sets of cutlery wrapped in linen napkins, and then presented each of the guests with a covered dish. "What should I do with Mrs. Ashcroft's plate?" he asked.

"Leave it here, George," Marjorie directed. "She should be back shortly."

"Shall I lift the covers?"

"Oh, that won't be necessary. We'll wait for Mrs. Ashcroft to return," Miller replied. "Thank you, George."

George nodded and trudged back to the house. As he scaled the front steps, Griselda emerged through the front door, glass in one hand and cocktail shaker in the other.

"There she is," Marjorie indicated.

George lent Griselda his arm as she lurched and reeled down the steps and across the lawn.

"Look at the state of her," Miller said, aghast.

"She is a mess isn't she? Poor thing."

"Poor thing?" Miller repeated. "She should be in bed."

"Not yet. We'll let her have her dinner, Mr. Miller. Like I said, it may sober her up. But if she's still in bad shape, afterwards, I'll put her straight to bed," Marjorie guaranteed. "And in her room, not mine. Heaven knows, I listened to enough of her nattering last night."

George helped Griselda onto the wrought-iron bench seat and uncovered her dinner.

"Thank you, George. You're a good boy," Griselda slobbered as she rubbed his arm somewhat seductively. "And a strong one too."

"Griselda," Marjorie said sharply. "Let George go back to the house so we can eat our dinner."

As a bemused George made his leave, Marjorie mouthed a silent apology.

"Dinner?" Griselda said absently and then proceeded to look down at her plate. "Oh, doesn't that look delicious!" she exclaimed and held the plate aloft for Marjorie to see.

"Yes, I know, dear," Marjorie replied. "We each have one just like it."

Griselda put the plate back down with a loud clink and dug into the contents with her fork. "Mmm, yummy!" she moaned and then smiled and pointed to her cocktail glass, "but not as yummy as this." She downed the balance of the Manhattan in one swig and then licked the inside of the glass before refilling it.

Miller picked at his poached red snapper with orange sauce and Bermuda style rice and peas, and watched in annoyed silence as Griselda alternated between making love to her cocktail glass, chewing her food noisily, tearing up at the memory of her beloved "Richie," and nodding off.

It was dusk by the time George finished clearing away the dirty dishes.

"I'm going to powder my nose," Marjorie announced as she pushed away from the table. "Griselda, would you care to come with me?"

Griselda, startled, looked up. "What? Um, no . . . but if you're going inside, would you be a dear and mix me some more Manhattans?"

"I think you've had enough Manhattans for now, Griselda," Marjorie opined. "Why don't we get you to bed?"

"I don't want to go to bed," Griselda

replied belligerently. "I want to see the fire-works."

Marjorie leaned over Griselda and helped her up from the bench. "You can see the fireworks. Take a little nap now and I'll wake you when they're about to start."

"Really?" Griselda slurred and draped herself on Marjorie's shoulder. "You know something? You're the best friend I've ever had."

Marjorie grinned and shook her head.

"No, I mean it," Griselda maintained. "Nobody other than my sister has treated me as good as you do."

Miller rose from his chair. "Do you need a hand?"

"No, I'm fine," Marjorie assured. "George is inside if I need help getting her upstairs."

Miller sat back down. "All right. I'll keep the wine chilled for the fireworks."

"Thanks."

"Wine?" Griselda spoke up. "That sounds peachy! Save me some, will ya?"

"Oh, don't worry. We'll save you some, all right," Marjorie quipped as she urged Griselda forward.

When they were a safe distance from Miller, Griselda whispered, "How did I do?"

"Beautifully," Marjorie whispered in reply. "I was starting to think you weren't acting.

And those Manhattans looked . . . well, like Manhattans."

"That's because they were Manhattans," Griselda answered as she staggered on toward the house. "Weak ones. But how's about explaining why I'm doing this? All I know is you came back from searching for the whistle and slipped a note in to my hand asking me to pretend to get gassed. What gives?"

"I figured out who did it. I know who killed Cassandra and your husband and, more importantly, I know why."

"Well, don't leave me hanging. Who did it?"

"Miller," Marjorie stated plainly.

"What?" Griselda shrieked. "You mean I ate dinner with a —"

"Shh! He'll hear you," Marjorie quieted. "It all fell into place when I went to get the whistle and saw George staring out the office window."

"Am I supposed to be able to figure that out?"

"The night your husband was murdered, I found Miller in the office and asked him if he had seen Creighton. He said he hadn't seen a soul, but when I left the office and went outside I —"

"Stumbled into me," Griselda recalled.

"And Creighton. The two of you had been outside for several minutes. If Miller had been in the office as long as he claimed, he would have spotted one of you out there or, at the very least, have seen you leave. If there's one thing you do well, Griselda, it's to command attention — be it making an entrance or an exit."

"No, if he were in the office, he definitely would have heard me," Griselda giggled. "But I still don't get it. So, he lied about being in the office — what does it mean?"

"On its own, not much," Marjorie confessed. "But when added to the elaborate plot to get the Ashcrofts to Bermuda, my 'sleeping sickness,' and the missing whistle, well . . ." Griselda stared blankly at Marjorie as they wended their way up the steps that led to the front door.

"Here's what happened," Marjorie explained. "Miller was, more or less, a part of your household, was he not?"

"Well, he had dinner with us most evenings, yes."

Marjorie nodded. "As such, Miller knew that Prudence was on Seconal; and probably knew exactly where she kept it too (Pru isn't exactly a tight-lipped sort of girl). He also knew about your husband's evening habit of drinking two glasses of brandy.

Maybe he'd even served it to him once or twice before leaving for the night. And, finally, he knew of this place — the house at Black Island — although he had never personally been here. Indeed, none of Mr. Ashcroft's secretaries — other than you, Griselda — had ever set eyes on the place. Why? Because it's here that 'Richie' and the first Mrs. Ashcroft came to escape from the world at large."

"You're right, Richie never did business here," Griselda stated.

"And Miller knew that. However, that didn't change the fact that he had been ordered to get here."

"Ordered? Who ordered him?"

"We'll get to that later," Marjorie dismissed. "But get here Miller must, so he fabricates the meeting with the representative of English Steel, thereby ensuring that your husband, and Edward, will be here for the week of the regatta, and also ensuring that he will be taken along on the trip — after all, a merger of that size would generate a great deal of paperwork. The only problem is that your husband isn't Miller's only employer, and paperwork isn't his sole raison d'être. No, Miller's agenda requires that your husband be . . . let us say, 'out of the way' for several hours at a time."

"So," Marjorie continued as she opened the front door and guided Griselda into the foyer, "he uses the knowledge he has to 'get the old man out of his hair.' He steals a handful of Pru's Seconal and adds it to the decanter of brandy, safe in the knowledge that no one else here drinks the stuff. Only —"

"Only Richie fired him," Griselda filled in the blank.

"Exactly," Marjorie frowned. "Leaving Miller just a few short hours in which to carry out his orders. He drugs your husband and sets about his business according to plan, but when he can't find what he's looking for and 'Richie' wakes up, he . . ."

Griselda put her hand to her mouth.

"Miller kills him and puts him in the trunk in order to delay the body's discovery and buy himself enough time to find what he's looking for," Marjorie concluded.

"But what is he looking for?" Griselda asked as they climbed the stairs to the second floor.

"The drawings for the new airplane. Your husband knew how valuable, and dangerous, they could be if they fell into the wrong hands. That's why he worked on them at home, late at night. For all we know, he may have even sensed something odd about Mil-

270

ler, but couldn't quite place the source of his concern."

"Who does Miller work for?" Griselda asked, her voice filled with fear.

"I can't say exactly, but some European government. You see," Marjorie elaborated, "the first night I met him, I thought Miller was English, like the rest of the Ashcrofts. He didn't have the accent, but there was something about him that gave me that impression. Looking back on that night, I realize it was the suit. I believe they call it —"

"The London Drape? I've seen it in my magazines; it's been the rage in Europe, and it's making its way into Hollywood."

"Yes, but even though the 'Drape' has made it to this side of the Atlantic, it's still wildly expensive, especially for a mere secretary. That's when it dawned on me: Miller didn't pay for it. Whoever outfitted Mr. Miller spared no expense in positioning him as the perfect gentleman's gentleman."

"It's just a suit," Griselda argued. "Hardly proof that he's foreign."

"It's not just the suit," Marjorie went on. "Last night, I saw Miller in the kitchen, eating supper. He held his utensils in the European manner; never switching hands, but pushing his food onto the back of his fork with his knife."

"So you think Miller is a — a spy? Oh, Gawd," Griselda exclaimed. "What are we going to do?"

"That, my dear Griselda, is why you had to pretend to be drunk. I needed a reason to come back inside." The two women had reached the upstairs hallway. "Miller hangs around this place like a moth around an incandescent bulb. Now that we're alone in the house, I'm going to look for the drawings, while you stand watch."

"But why not go to the police?"

"The police won't believe a word I say unless I can prove that the drawings were here, in the house," Marjorie explained. "Now, quit yapping and stand at the top of the steps, while I go search your bedroom. If you hear or see anything, come in and get me. We'll act as though I was trying to put you to bed."

Griselda nodded in agreement, then, her eyes, welling with tears, said, "Marjorie?"

"What?"

"I'm scared," Griselda threw her arms around Marjorie and embraced her.

"I am too, Gris," Marjorie admitted. "I am too."

TWENTY-NINE

"That's terrific, Mr. Beaufort," Edward said into the telephone receiver. "I appreciate all you've done to get the money together. I can't thank you enough . . . Yes, I'll be sure to give you the information regarding any services . . . I will, sir . . . yes, and I'll send my best to Creighton and Prudence . . . oh, Prudence and I will be certain to visit you and your wife when we get back . . . Thank you again, sir . . . Good night to you, too."

Edward hung up the phone and ran to his brother's cell. "Well, after hours of battling bureaucracy, you're finally a free man."

"And none too soon, I may add. Another day here, and I'd look like him," Creighton nodded toward the bearded man in the adjacent cell. "Probably smell like him, too. How'd you manage to pull it off?"

"I called the bank president, Henry Beaufort. You remember him, don't you? He belongs to father's club; they were always trying to match you up with Beaufort's daughter —"

"Ah yes, Helen 'Horseface' Beaufort," Creighton smiled. "How could I possibly forget?"

"Beaufort hasn't forgotten either," Edward explained. "Especially the 'Horseface' part."

"I told you, I didn't know it was Beaufort."

"It was a costume ball, Creighton. One would have thought you'd have exercised a bit more caution before telling the fellow at the buffet table that your father's friend 'owed you one' for taking his daughter out of the 'corral' that evening."

"The 'fellow' you described was wearing a gorilla suit; I thought I was safe. Never, in my wildest dreams, would I have believed that a bank president would dress up like a monkey, especially in a room filled with wealthy investors," Creighton argued. "No wonder banks are failing left and right."

"Just the same, I thought it best not to tell him that the money was to bail you out of jail," Edward stated.

"Wise decision," Creighton approved.

With that, the telephone rang. It was answered by the fresh-faced constable who had been left to tend to the station while the remaining constables on duty walked the streets surrounding the harbor, just in case the evening's festivities got out of hand.

"Hamilton Police Station, hallo? . . . A who? From where? . . . Detective Robert Jameson from the States? I don't know 'im . . . Why, yes, we do have a Creighton Ashcroft here, but the prisoner isn't allowed phone calls."

"Wait!" Creighton shouted from his cell. "My brother has the bail money."

"Hold on, please," the constable spoke into the receiver and then covered the mouthpiece with his hand. "I can't release you," he explained to Creighton. "You need to pay the bail at the courthouse tomorrow morning."

"Fine," Creighton agreed. "But, at least let me take that call."

"Sorry, but I can't do that."

"Then let my brother take the call," Creighton went on, "But he's going to share the information with me anyway."

The constable pulled a face and uncovered the mouthpiece. "Yes, we'll accept the call." While waiting for the connection, he placed the receiver down on his desk and unlocked the door of Creighton's cell.

Creighton rushed forward and snatched the telephone receiver from its spot on the desk. "Hello? Hello, Jameson?"

"Hi, Creighton," Jameson's voice greeted.

275

"How's prison life treating you?"

"You know, Jameson, it's amazing how even from a distance of one thousand miles, I can find you utterly annoying."

"Then my job is done," Jameson laughed. "Listen, I have that information Marjorie requested."

"Well, Marjorie's not here, so I'm going to have to suffice."

"She's not there? With her powers of persuasion, I would have thought she'd have gotten the police there to fix her up in the cell next to yours."

Creighton glanced at the bearded man sleeping in the middle cell. "No, that cell was already . . . occupied."

"Oh, that would explain it," Jameson said. "So, here's what I've got. First, that telegram that your brother received upon arriving in Bermuda, confirming his and Richard's appointment?"

"Yes?" Creighton urged.

"It was sent from New York, not Hamilton. It was ordered on August 16 with explicit instructions that it not be sent to Bermuda until the nineteenth."

Creighton addressed Edward, "When did you, Pru, and Cassandra arrive on Black Island?"

"The nineteenth. Why?" Edward asked.

Creighton shook his head and went back to his telephone conversation. "The nineteenth was the day of my brother's arrival. Sounds like whoever sent it was familiar with his itinerary."

"Hmm," Jameson remarked. "Since it was such an odd request, the telegraph agent remembered the person who ordered it: a woman with long, black hair. Exotic looking."

"Cassandra," Creighton thought aloud.

"Cassandra? Isn't that the name of the second person who was murdered?" Jameson asked.

"Yes, it was. That's why it's so surprising."

"Well, it gets even better. I checked out Cassandra, a.k.a. Rose, and there is absolutely no record of a spiritual whatchamacallit having ripped off some old woman in Rhode Island, not under the name Cassandra, Rose, or any other name. Either the person who told you that story got his places mixed up, or the story is completely fabricated."

"That is interesting," Creighton remarked, "because the teller of that tale was my deceased father and if there was something he always did, it was check his facts."

"Maybe," Jameson replied, "but his secretary is a bit of a mystery."

"You mean, Miller?"

"If that's what he wants to call himself, sure," Jameson allowed. "It seems to work insofar as his business references go, but I hit a wall when I checked into his college education."

"What do you mean?" Creighton asked for clarification.

"I mean that Herman Miller didn't graduate from Lafayette College in 1920, but Hermann Müller did. He majored in English literature and was a member of the Industrial Workers of the World, along with other Socialist organizations."

"Our Miller claimed to have been writing the Great American novel when he decided to become a secretary," Creighton explained to Jameson. "You think they're one and the same?"

"After what I unearthed about Müller and the war, I'm willing to bet on it," Jameson stated.

"The war? As a German living in America, I'm sure Müller faced persecution, but that should have lessened considerably by 1920. The war ended two years before."

"The war ended in 1918, yes," Jameson corrected. "But the Germans didn't sign the Treaty until 1919."

"So?"

"So, according to Müller's school records, in his junior year, he was suspended for organizing a rally to protest the Treaty of Versailles and the blockade imposed upon Germany until their acceptance of the Treaty's conditions." Jameson went on, "In his senior year, he started a petition to end the war reparations being paid by Germany to the Allies — namely Great Britain and France — and submitted a political cartoon to the school newspaper depicting a woman, Germany, tied to a stake with ropes labeled as 'The Treaty.' Since neither deed violated any rules, the school took no action against Müller; however, they took note of the events because of their disruptive potential."

"Disruptive is putting it mildly. Considering that many of Müller's fellow students had probably lost friends and family during the war, I'm certain they weren't overly pleased at having a German nationalist running about campus," Creighton noted.

"I'm sure many of them were offended and possibly even outraged," Jameson agreed. "But I'm also sure that more than a few of them laughed at the irony of that particular German nationalist's name."

"Hermann Müller? What's so — ? Ah, wait a minute. He was . . ." the answer was in the forefront of Creighton's memory, but he couldn't quite articulate it. "He was . . ."

"One of the German delegates who signed the Treaty," Jameson answered his own question.

"I would have come up with that answer eventually," Creighton said peevishly.

"Sorry. I wanted to cut to the chase."

Creighton grunted. "You're right, that explains the name change. But how does it fit with the case?"

"I don't know. Marjorie told me the names of the victims and then asked me to fill in the blanks she found particularly suspicious, that's all."

"Thanks, Jameson," Creighton said appreciatively. "You did an excellent job 'filling in the blanks.' Let us know how we can repay you for all your hard work."

"For starters, you can take care of this telephone bill," Jameson stated bluntly. "If the Chief gets wind that I called Bermuda from the station phone, he'll have my badge."

"I'll take care of it as soon as I'm back," Creighton promised.

"Thanks, and I'm sorry about the jail time crack," Jameson apologized. "That's an awful way to spend a honeymoon."

"It certainly is," Creighton agreed.

"Well, hurry back to that beautiful bride

280

of yours, and next time you take a honeymoon, stay in the States," Jameson advised. "That way I can be a better help when you inevitably run into a dead body."

"Good night, Jameson," Creighton responded crabbily.

"Good night, Creighton. Safe home." There was a loud click as Jameson disconnected.

Creighton replaced the receiver onto its cradle and turned to his brother. "So, tell me, Edward, what was Father working on when he was killed?"

THIRTY

Marjorie entered the Ashcrofts' darkened bedroom and rushed toward the bed. In the years since the crash, Marjorie had heard various accounts of people who, motivated by distrust and fear, placed their life savings under mattresses.

Could Ashcroft, also motivated by distrust and fear, have used the same device to guard the plans for the new airplane?

Frantically, Marjorie pulled back the bedspread and thrust her arm, as far as it would go, between the mattress and boxspring. Quickly, yet systematically, she moved around the edges of the bed, feeling the dark recess for any sign of paper. She found none.

Had Ashcroft taped the drawings to the underside of the mattress? Marjorie wondered.

No, she determined. Given their potential significance, Ashcroft would have checked

282

the drawings regularly in order to ensure both their safety and validity. The process of undoing the bed, lifting the mattress, and removing the tape, would have been impractical. In addition, sharing a room with Griselda afforded him neither the time nor the privacy to engage in such a complicated process.

Perhaps he kept them in the bed, under the covers? Marjorie stood up, pulled back the covers and checked between the top sheet and blanket. Nothing.

She was not surprised; even if Ashcroft kept them on his side of the bed, Griselda would have noticed them through the thin summer blanket.

Maybe her theory about the bed was wrong, she thought. Ashcroft may simply have been particular about his bedding, although Marjorie thought it an unusual quirk for a man of his wealth and status. Where, precisely, would Ashcroft, a man who had spent his entire life surrounded by servants, have picked up such a habit? Although it wasn't impossible, it didn't fit with the man she had met.

She picked up the closest pillow and gave it and the starched white pillowcase enclosing it a close examination. Again, nothing. She threw it down and placed a palm onto the mattress to brace herself, leaning across the bed for the other pillow. It was then that she noticed that the section of the mattress upon which she was leaning was slightly firmer than the rest.

Marjorie stood up and felt the area; with her fingers, she could trace the outline of an object, flat and rectangular. However, it was not directly beneath the sheet, but farther down. Hastily, she untucked the bottom sheet and pulled back the mattress pad.

"Gris!" Marjorie called in a loud whisper. "Griselda!"

Marjorie's platinum blonde accomplice appeared in the doorway. "Did you find it?" she asked excitedly.

"Yes, it's here," Marjorie held the series of reduced-scale blueprints aloft for Griselda to see. Neither woman knew much about airplanes and even less about engineer's drawings, but they both understood that the inclusion of guns in the design meant that this aircraft was for military use, rather than civilian passenger conveyance.

"So that's it," Griselda noted sadly. "That's the reason Richie was killed. Because of some stupid pieces of paper."

"He won't be the last," Marjorie responded. "Especially if these plans become reality."

"Men," Griselda uttered in disgust. "Always trying to find new ways to kill each other. Didn't they get it out of their systems with the last war?"

"If history is any indication, no." Marjorie replaced the mattress pad and sheet, and smoothed them down. "Okay, shut the door and put on your nightgown," she instructed Griselda. "This way if Miller comes into the house, it looks like I've actually been putting you to bed. I'm going to fold up the drawings so that I can smuggle them out of here."

Griselda nodded and changed into a purple silk negligee. Meanwhile, Marjorie folded the drawings into as small a square as possible and anchored it inside the strap of her brassiere.

"Ha!" Griselda laughed as she watched Marjorie hide the drawings. "My mother did the same thing, but her stash was money. Money she snuck away from Pop."

"Go to bed," Marjorie teased.

Griselda obediently slid between the covers and sighed. "I'm so glad that's over."

"I am, too. Well, that part of it at least."

"What do you mean, 'that part of it'?"

"Now that I have the drawings, I need to get them to the police."

"When are you planning to do that?"

Griselda asked.

"As soon as I can get away from Miller," Marjorie explained. "If he's downstairs, waiting for me to join him for the fireworks, then I'll meet Constable Smith after Miller's gone to bed."

"Be careful," Griselda warned. "And come back later, will ya? Just to let me know you're okay. Please?"

"I will," Marjorie replied and took off down the hallway, just as a loud boom resonated though the limestone dwelling, shaking the windows and rattling the doors. The fireworks had begun.

Marjorie hastened down the cedar staircase, pausing to catch her breath in front of the heavily carved front door. Outside, Miller waited. *You can do this,* she told herself. *You've made it this far. Stay calm just a little while longer.*

She swung open the door and made her way down the front steps, all the while keeping an eye on the shimmering pyrotechnics going off high in the sky above Hamilton Harbor.

As she headed down the gravel path just a few yards from the table, a fountain of blue and gold sparks illuminated the heavens. "Ohhhh," Marjorie commented loudly. "That was pretty!"

She needn't have bothered. Although the table, benches and glasses of wine were exactly as she had left them, Miller was nowhere to be seen.

After a quick scan of the lawn and the neighboring woods, Marjorie hastened down the path toward the cove where Constable Smith was standing guard. She knew she had to hand the drawings off to the police and present her story as compellingly as possible; then, and only then, would she be safe.

She had just reached the top of the stairs when she encountered the black cat meowing and crying and pacing back and forth.

"It's okay, puss," Marjorie said soothingly. "The fireworks will be over before long, but right now, I have work to do." She leaned down and tried to scratch the feline behind the ears, but the cat would have none of it. With a swat and a loud hiss, he took off into the darkness.

Marjorie stood up and rubbed at the claw marks on the back of her hand. She should have known better than to try to pet an agitated cat. Still, his reaction had taken her by surprise. She shook her head, removed her shoes, and descended the cliff wall stairs.

In the flickering light of the fireworks, she could pick out the figure of Constable

Smith, seated on the pier, his back resting against one of the tall wooden pilings.

"Constable Smith," she called.

The policeman didn't move.

"Constable Smith," she said, in a louder voice this time. "I need your help."

Again, the policeman did not respond.

Marjorie placed a hand on his shoulder and gave him a gentle shake. "Constable Smith?"

The movement sent Constable Smith's hat tumbling onto the sand, thus revealing a small, round bullet hole in the center of his forehead.

Marjorie backed away in horror. Not only had Smith been killed, but dangling from the piling against which he rested, was the missing whistle.

She opened her mouth to scream, but before she could make a sound, a searing pain shot from the base of her skull to the top of head.

The world around her grew dark . . .

THIRTY-ONE

Sergeant Jackson stormed through the doors of the Hamilton Police Station. "This had better be good," he threatened. "Mrs. Jackson made a leg of lamb and spotted dick for supper."

"Sounds a right treat," Creighton remarked, hungrily. "Anniversary?"

"It was awful," Jackson responded. "If I didn't know better, I'd think she was trying to kill me. But she tries so hard."

"To kill you?" Creighton teased.

"To cook something I'll like," Jackson said angrily. "Now then, which one of you monkeys had the bright idea to telephone me?"

Edward and Creighton both turned to look at the young constable.

"It — it was me, sir," the youth raised his hand. "The Ashcrofts here were trying to get back to Black Island."

"So, let them," Jackson replied breezily.

289

"They won't get far on a night like tonight."

"You're right," Edward confessed. "We didn't. We can't cross the harbor without a police escort."

"Which is why we came back here," Creighton added. "And why we had the Constable call you. We need to get across, now. Tonight."

"You're a prisoner," Jackson scoffed. "You're not going anywhere, except back to your cell."

"I have the bail money," Edward stated.

"Well, isn't that lovely? You can bring it by the courthouse tomorrow morning."

"It can't wait until tomorrow morning," Creighton argued. "My wife may be in danger."

"From what? Boredom?"

"Herman Miller," Creighton stated. "We have reason to believe he's a German agent."

"What? Oh, Mr. Ashcroft," Jackson laughed. "Surely, you can come up with something better than that."

"Wait, Sergeant," the constable pleaded. "Just hear them out."

"They've got you, too, have they, Constable?" Jackson chuckled as he pulled over a chair from a nearby desk and sat in it. "All right, go ahead. Convince me."

"As you know, our family's business specializes in aircraft parts and design," Creighton explained. "At the time of his murder, my father was in the midst of designing a new fighter plane. A fighter plane capable of reaching unprecedented speeds but still retaining maneuverability."

"Obviously, an airplane of that caliber would appeal to a great many people. So, although the idea was to keep the design top secret, it wasn't long before news of my father's work leaked," Edward continued. "He began receiving letters and visits from various foreign dignitaries, all seeking to purchase the plans. But two of these, shall we say, 'special interest groups,' were especially tenacious."

"The Germans," Jackson guessed.

"Hmm, and the Russians," Edward added. "They were willing to pay any price to gain possession of my father's plans."

"And he didn't take them up on the offer?"

"Our father may have been many things, Sergeant, but a traitor wasn't one of them. As a resident of the United States, he pitched the plane to America first; when they turned him down, he took them to the British who, in turn, paid him handsomely to continue development."

"I don't see how this relates to Miller or the murders," Jackson stated.

"Both the Germans and the Russians were relentless. Until, that is, a few months ago. Since then, nothing," Edward related.

"They didn't go away, they simply tried a different approach," Creighton explained. "One Herman Miller, or more correctly, Müller, a German nationalist who grew up in the States but holds a grudge against the Allies for their treatment of his motherland. The Germans trained him to be a secretary; they even provided him with exemplary references."

"The only problem," Edward chimed in, "is that, as a secretary, Miller only has access to the office and the more public areas of the family home. Father, however, never kept important documents in his office or even in the safe. He always kept them close at hand so he could watch them."

"That's why Miller made the phony appointment," Jackson concluded. "So he'd be living under the same roof with Ashcroft and the plans."

"And the Regatta gave him a chance to meet with his German contacts without suspicion," Creighton elaborated.

"But if he knew the appointment was a fake, why did he send a telegram confirming it?" Jackson questioned.

"He didn't," Creighton replied. "Cassandra did."

"Cassandra? Why?"

"She wanted both my father and Miller out of the house at the same time. I believe it was so that she could search for the drawings herself."

"The spiritual guide business wasn't lucrative enough for her?"

"Umm, about that," Creighton added. "Detective Jameson couldn't find anything about her having cheated a woman out of her inheritance. Which means that either she was highly successful at keeping a low profile or the story was inaccurate."

"It can't be inaccurate," Jackson stated. "It came from your father."

"The announcement might have come from my father, but the information didn't. My father wouldn't have done that research himself — he saved his very limited patience for drawings and things of that nature — he had Miller do the legwork. And Miller used that opportunity to try to get Cassandra out of the way."

"But if Cassandra wasn't a grifter, who was —" Jackson started to ask, and then remembered the necklace found near the body. "Cassandra was a Russian agent," he concluded. "And Miller knew it. That's why he murdered her."

"How do you — ?" Creighton started.

"I'll explain in the boat," Jackson dismissed curtly. "Right now we're heading to Black Island."

The three men rushed to the door, only to be greeted by Inspector Nettles, who was on his way inside. "Say, I had that brandy decanter examined by a doctor friend of mine and Marjorie's right. It does contain Seconal."

"We know," Jackson pushed Nettles aside both literally and figurative.

"How do you know?"

"We'll explain on the way there."

"The way where?"

"Black Island. We're going to catch ourselves a killer."

THIRTY-TWO

Marjorie awoke to the hum of a motor and the sensation of movement. She opened her eyes to find herself slumped into the passenger seat of the speedster, her upper torso draped over the side of the boat and her head hovering a few inches above the water.

Ignoring the searing pain in her skull, Marjorie turned her head slightly to the left and watched as the speedster pulled away from Black Island. In the flickering light cast by the fireworks overhead, she could see the figure of a young man descend the cliff-side staircase, pause by Smith's body, and then run across the beach.

It was George.

Don't do it, she thought as she watched him wade into the cove. *George, don't do it!* Marjorie lifted her head to scream, but quickly realized that doing so would seal the boy's fate.

As if he could hear her pleas, George ran

back to the shore and scrambled up the cliff-side steps.

Thank goodness, Marjorie sighed in relief.

"Welcome back, Mrs. Ashcroft," Miller said over the sound of the motor. "And thank you for the drawings."

Marjorie sat up, tentatively, and felt beneath the left strap of her brassiere. As expected, the drawings were gone. She shuddered, partly because she had come too far on this journey to let Miller take possession of the plans, and partly because Miller had searched her person in order to find them.

"You're tougher than you look," he went on, "I thought for certain you wouldn't come to until we were in Hamilton."

"Why . . ." she started, but the sound of her own voice caused excruciating pain.

"Why are you still alive?" Miller ventured.

She nodded slowly.

"Insurance. I'm boarding a boat out of Hamilton tonight and I don't want anyone to stop me."

Marjorie drew a deep breath. Here, in the cove, surrounded by the walls of Black Island, she and Miller were cut off from civilization, but ahead, in Hamilton Harbor, there would be other boats: fishing boats, harbor master patrol boats, boats that

296

dropped anchor to watch the fireworks. All she would need to do is get the attention of those boats and . . .

Her heart sunk with the realization that the flare gun that might have been used to signal the attention of other boats had been left ashore, flares exhausted, by Creighton and Edward during their efforts to signal the attention of the police.

The lights of Hamilton's Front Street shimmered and danced upon the water, outshined only by the occasional rocket flare, and so close as to seem almost tangible. Marjorie closed her eyes to shield herself from their taunts and tried to plan her next move.

Should she swim? Should she scream? Should she try to push Miller overboard? They were all viable options, but the success of any of them depended upon one inextricable truth: she needed to get to the harbor. And here, in the shallows surrounding the island, progress was slow at best.

"So I'm a hostage?" Marjorie finally asked.

"I prefer to call it a prisoner of war."

"We're not at war," she pointed out.

"Not yet, but we will be," Miller said confidently. "In the next war, Deutschland will take its proper place in the world and those who betrayed her will be vanquished."

"The day of reckoning," Marjorie muttered.

"Mr. Ashcroft showed you that note, did he? Sloppy of me to have dropped it in the office, but I was in a hurry."

"Of course! You wrote it to let your cronies know that you arrived at Black Island according to plan. When you murdered Ashcroft, you removed it from his pocket, just in case the police could lift the fingerprints. And the key . . ."

"Go on," Miller urged. "Let's see if you can figure it out."

"The key was never in his pocket," Marjorie deduced. "We only had your word that it was ever there in the first place."

"Clever girl. Keep going."

"When you couldn't find the drawings, you wondered if Ashcroft had, indeed, brought them along. Not wanting to take any chances, you sent the key to your cronies so that they could safely investigate Ashcroft's office while he and his family were out of town." Marjorie's eyes grew wide. "That's what you were stuffing into the envelope that night. It wasn't your resume; it was the key and a set of instructions."

"Excellent," Miller proclaimed loudly. "It's a shame you aren't on our side."

298

"I still haven't figured out why *you* aren't on *ours*," she countered.

Miller flashed a wry smile. "Why am I not on the side of a people who gave me regular beatings during the war? Why am I not on the side of a people who fired my father from his job at the mill? Why am I not on the side of a people who posted signs prohibiting us from certain parts of town, while welcoming only 'loyal Americans'? Loyal Americans who didn't like the sound of our last name.

"We could have taken the easy way out. Could have changed our name. But my father," Miller continued, "wouldn't think of it, not while there was breath in his body. He was proud to be German, and he didn't want us to forget that we were German too. After the war, he considered going back to Deutschland, but it was too late. The reparations that you and your Allies demanded had forced my homeland into economic ruin. My aunts and uncles were poverty-stricken and inflation was such that my parents' life savings would have been just enough to support them for a week."

They were entering the narrow part of the cove. Once through, they would be in Hamilton Harbor.

Marjorie watched as Miller rose in his seat

in order to gauge the boat's clearance. As she did so she could have sworn she saw something behind Miller slip from the shore into the water. *I'm seeing things,* Marjorie determined. *It's that blow to the head.*

What was real, however, was the pistol resting, directly beside Miller, on the driver's seat. *If only she could distract him . . .*

"You changed your name, though," she stated. "To disguise who you really were."

"I disguise who I am," Miller asserted as they left Black Island behind, "not because I'm ashamed, but because I wish to deliver justice. I wish to —"

In an instant, George emerged from the water and put Miller in a strangle hold. As the two men struggled, Marjorie sprung from her seat and seized the pistol from the driver's side of the cockpit, but not before Miller could deliver a swift kick to her chin.

The force of the blow sent the gun flying onto the rear deck of the boat and launched Marjorie overboard.

Marjorie felt herself sink beneath the inky depths of Hamilton Harbor. Clawing, kicking, and grasping at her watery surroundings, she endeavored to fight her way to the surface, but the wake created by the motor of the speedster kept pulling her under.

Please, God, she prayed. *Please God, don't*

let me drown.

As if by way of a miracle, the surrounding waters began to glow with a brilliant white light. Marjorie wondered if she might be dying until she saw a pair of arms break through the surface of the water and reach toward her.

With a kick of her legs, she propelled herself closer to the outstretched arms and held on tightly while they pulled her out of the harbor and dragged her into a dilapidated fishing boat. Marjorie gasped and coughed as Creighton held her in his arms and Edward wrapped her in a blanket.

"Thank God you're all right," Creighton said, tears welling in his eyes.

Marjorie nodded. "But George," she rasped.

"We know."

Marjorie looked up to see the bright lights of the fishing boat focused on the idling speedster and the two figures upon its rear deck.

Jackson moved to the bow of the fishing boat and announced through a large megaphone, "Stop! Police!"

George lay upon his back, hands in the air, while Miller, brandishing the gun, stood over him.

"Put the gun down and let the boy go,"

Jackson demanded

Miller replied by cocking the pistol and aiming it at George's head.

"What's that going to get you?" Jackson challenged. "Are you going to shoot all of us as well? Are you going to shoot your way through town? That's what it will take for you to get out of this."

"I will not dishonor my family name or my country by turning myself in," Miller shouted in reply. "I will not be called a failure."

The two boats were close enough for Marjorie to see the deathly pallor and pained expression of the German agent's face.

He looked at Marjorie and said, "In the next war, only the strong will survive. It appears, Frau Ashcroft, that you will be there and I will not."

With that, Miller put the barrel of the gun in his mouth and pulled the trigger.

THIRTY-THREE

A day passed before Marjorie's agonizing headache finally abated and she left her darkened bedroom to follow her husband downstairs for breakfast.

"You seemed eager to get me out of bed this morning," she said to Creighton. "What are you up to?"

"Surprises, darling. Surprises."

"Ohhhh, I think we've had enough surprises for now."

"But not good ones." Creighton opened the front door and directed her view to the front lawn.

There, at the same table Marjorie had shared with Miller, the Ashcrofts — both established and newly discovered — had assembled.

"Are you going to tell — ?" Marjorie asked excitedly.

"You'll see," Creighton said impatiently. "Now let's go. Everyone's waiting."

They wended their way to the table where Selina greeted each of them with a glass of orange juice mixed with champagne and grenadine. "Everything is set up just as you requested," Selina whispered to Creighton, who responded with a single nod of the head.

He helped Marjorie into her seat.

Marjorie glanced around the table and paused at one familiar face. "Pru? When did you get out of the hospital?"

"Yesterday. Edward brought me back home." She smiled happily at her husband, who appeared genuinely pleased at her return.

"And we both agreed to no more pills," Edward added.

Marjorie smiled. "I'm very glad to hear that."

Creighton stood behind his wife, his glass held high.

"Ladies and gentlemen," he announced, "it's been an interesting past few days, but we've survived and, thankfully, have grown closer and learned more about each other because of it." As the group toasted their newfound unity, Creighton mouthed a silent acknowledgement to Selina.

"As you all know," Creighton continued, "I was named as the sole beneficiary of my father's will. I, however, don't believe that's very fair. It's not what Edward and my mother would have wanted.

"Selina," he went on, "you've given this family so much over the years, including (with your story yesterday) a chance for Edward and I to better understand our parents. Therefore, Edward and I want Black Island to be in your name."

Selina's jaw dropped. "What? You mean . . . ?"

"The house, the trees, the cove, it's all yours," Edward explained.

"We just ask that you'll allow us to visit from time to time," Creighton rejoined with a laugh.

"Of course you can," Selina exclaimed. "It — it wouldn't be the same without you boys here. All you boys."

George embraced his mother and pumped Creighton's hand furiously. "You've made my mother a happy woman. I don't know what to say."

"You might tell us what you'd like to do with your life," Creighton suggested.

"Do?"

"Well, certain colleges are known for their medical programs, others for law, and still others for business."

"Are you saying . . . ?" George questioned.

Selina, meanwhile, gasped and hugged her son.

"We're saying, George, that you're our brother," Creighton stated simply. "Even though there are some who may look upon you as a lesser brother, in our eyes, you're equal."

George reached his hand across the table and shook Edward's hand vigorously. "Mr. Edward, thank you. Thank so much."

"You're welcome. And, by the way, you can drop the 'Mr.'," Edward replied with a smile.

"I will, Mr. — I mean, Edward." George turned to Creighton and pumped his hand just as furiously as he had Edward's. "And thank you, Mr. Creighton. Thank you!"

"No, thank *you*," Marjorie piped in. "If it weren't for you, it might have been me looking down the barrel of that gun and things might not have ended so well. Although, I have to admit, I'm still not sure where you came from."

"It was that cat of yours," George said. "He was pacing back and forth by the steps. When I saw him, I figured something was wrong, so I went downstairs to investigate. I — I saw Constable Smith and then you in the boat with Miller. I knew I'd never catch up by swimming, so I went by foot and met

306

up with you by the neck of the cove."

"I don't care how you did it," Marjorie remarked. "I'm just glad you did."

"That makes two of us," Creighton added before turning his attention to the platinum blonde seated beside Marjorie. "Griselda!"

"Oh, boy," she muttered under her breath. "Here it comes."

"Don't be worried," Marjorie assured. "This is good news."

"You sure? Because the last time we were at a table like this, it didn't exactly end well for me."

"You'll think differently this time," Creighton promised. "Aside from playing a drunk —"

"Which you did brilliantly!" Marjorie noted.

"— my wife tells me you're a talented seamstress. That's why, if you're interested, we'd like to set you up with your own dress shop. Not just mending or alterations, but designing, sewing, and selling dresses. How would you feel about that?"

Griselda's eyes filled with tears. "How would I feel? My very own business. My own money . . . mine! I — I'm overwhelmed."

"And I'm overwhelmed that you helped me the way you did," Marjorie said. "So I guess that makes us even."

"Edward," Creighton addressed his brother. "You didn't think you'd leave this table empty-handed did you? You've helped father run the business for years now and, during those years, you've done a far better job than I ever could. Therefore, I'm signing father's shares of the business over to you."

"Thank you," Edward said.

"However, I'm also kicking you out of the family home."

Edward's face was a question. "What?"

"Griselda will be staying in the house, but you and Prudence need a fresh start. That's why I'm giving you the money to purchase your own home . . . with one stipulation."

"Certainly," Edward agreed. "What is it?"

"That you learn from our parents and don't throw a good thing away," Creighton glanced at Prudence. "I don't want to play a regular role in the business, but if you need to take time with your wife and future family," he winked at Pru, "give me a call and I'll fill in for you."

Edward nodded. "I will. And thank you, Creighton. I mean that."

"Thank you for bailing me out of jail."

"Any time."

"Yes, well, let's hope we never again need

308

to take you up on that offer," Creighton joked and, placing his hands on his wife's shoulders, announced: "And, last but not least, Marjorie."

Marjorie spun around to look at her husband. "Me? I already have everything I need. Except, perhaps, a way home."

"Already done." Creighton extracted two cruise ship tickets from his inside jacket pocket. "We leave day after tomorrow. But first, we have some unfinished business. Namely, this." He held Marjorie's left hand in the air.

"What? The wedding ring?" Marjorie questioned. "We said we'd buy one as soon as we got back home."

"Nope." Creighton shook his head. "Not anymore, we aren't. We're not going anywhere else until I put a ring on your finger. Not with your track record."

"Oh, but —"

"No arguing. This time, we're doing it right. Now, Griselda and Prudence are going to take you upstairs and George will meet you behind the house in an hour."

Griselda and Pru, having sequestered Marjorie in her bedroom with her garments for the day, ran off, giggling, to tend to their own attire. An hour later, Marjorie emerged from the house, wearing a white chiffon tea dress and a wide-brimmed white hat.

George, dressed in a crisp blue dress shirt and white trousers, met her with a bouquet of lilies and quietly led her through the forest. At her first sight of the white dress, Marjorie had her suspicions as to what was going to transpire, but the sight awaiting her at the end of the trail far exceeded anything she might have imagined. A grassy bluff overlooking the sea had, with the addition on a white arch, been transformed into a temporary altar.

"This is the spot my mother and I told you about," George whispered. "When Creighton told me what he wanted to do, I thought you two might want to get married on the top of the world."

Marjorie hugged George tightly and the two marched to the edge of the bluff where Creighton — looking more handsome than ever in a white linen suit and a black neck tie — and the minister stood waiting.

There, surrounded by their family, Sergeant and Mrs. Jackson, and Inspector Nettles, with the deep blue of the Atlantic behind them, Creighton and Marjorie Ashcroft exchanged their marriage vows for the second, and final, time.

THIRTY-FOUR

Ridgebury was abuzz with excitement as they awaited Marjorie and Creighton's homecoming. A tent, complete with a dance floor and strands of white lights, had been erected on the church fairgrounds and lined with two buffet tables bearing a variety of sweet and savory dishes. Opposite the buffet tables, an old Victrola stood at the ready to provide the evening's entertainment.

The Schutts, having demonstrated a change of heart, not only brought the Perfection Salad, but donated twenty folding chairs for the event. Reverend Price had written a special blessing. And Detective Jameson, partly to hear about the rest of the case and partly as a means to escape Sharon, had volunteered to collect the newlyweds from the passenger ship terminal. He would use his car radio to give the townsfolk ample notice of their arrival.

Mrs. Patterson was refilling the lemonade

jug when Officer Noon came barreling through the tent entrance. "I got him," he exclaimed jubilantly. "I finally got him! And not a moment too soon!"

"Oh, that's wonderful, Patrick!" Emily Patterson clapped her hands to gain the attention of the other revelers. "Everyone! Did you hear? Officer Noonan has captured the dangerous felon. Now we can celebrate Marjorie and Creighton's marriage in complete safety!"

Noonan tried in vain to quiet the elderly woman, but it was no use. The entire town let out a collective cheer.

"What would we ever do without you?" Mrs. Wilson cried.

"For once, someone on the police force was doing their job," Mr. Schutt said proudly.

The only voice of dissention came from Freddie, the fifteen-year-old boy who ran the soda fountain at the Ridgebury drug store. "Wait one minute!" he called. "Officer Noonan was on the green most of the day, and I didn't see him catch nothin' except for a cat in a box trap. And I don't even think that cat was a stray."

"You keep a civil tongue in your head, young man," Mrs. Patterson scolded.

"It's the truth. I swear." He reached

outside the tent entrance and brought in a cage, with Sam inside. "See?"

Noonan reached inside and held the cat protectively. "I can — I can explain."

"Explain?" Mr. Schutt shrieked.

"You mean he didn't catch the fiend who's been terrorizing us?" Mrs. Wilson asked in confusion.

"Officer Noonan, how could you lie to us?" Reverend Price accused. "Don't you realize how frightened we've all been?"

In the midst of the townsfolk's cries and murmurs, Marjorie, Creighton, and Jameson had returned and now stood, unnoticed, in the entrance of the tent. If their presence had gone undetected, however, the small black cat in Marjorie's arms had not. At the sight of the foreign cat, Sam hissed, leapt from Noonan's arms, and ran, hell for leather, out the opposite end of the tent.

"Not again!" Noonan cried and ran after the feline.

"Stop!" Mr. Schutt commanded. "We're not done with you!"

As the townspeople gave chase, Creighton said to Marjorie, "Are you thinking what I'm thinking?"

"That as crazy and chaotic as it may be, it's good to be home?" Marjorie guessed.

"That," Creighton agreed, "and that if

there is a next war, all we need do is unleash
this circus and the enemy will cry uncle in
no time."

ABOUT THE AUTHOR

Amy Patricia Meade graduated cum laude from New York Institute of Technology and currently works as a freelance technical writer. Amy lives with her husband, Steve, his daughter, Carrie, and their two cats, Scout and Boo. She enjoys travel, cooking, needlepoint, and entertaining friends and family, and is a member of Sisters in Crime.